PUFFIN BOOKS

Daggie Dogfoot

Dick King-Smith served in the Grenadier Guards during the Second World War, and afterwards spent twenty years as a farmer in Gloucestershire, the county of his birth. Many of his stories are inspired by his farming experiences. Later he taught at a village primary school. His first book, *The Fox Busters,* was published in 1978. Since then he has written a great number of children's books, including *The Sheep-Pig* (winner of the *Guardian* Award and filmed as *Babe*), *Harry's Mad, Noah's Brother, The Hodgeheg, Martin's Mice, Ace, The Cuckoo Child* and *Harriet's Hare* (winner of the Children's Book Award in 1995). At the British Book Awards in 1992 he was voted Children's Author of the Year. He is married, with three children and eleven grandchildren, and lives in a seventeenth-century cottage a short crow's flight from the house where he w

DICK KING-SMITH

DAGGIE DOGFOOT

Illustrated by Mike Terry

PUFFIN BOOKS

PUFFIN BOOKS

Published by the Penguin Group
Penguin Books Ltd, 27 Wrights Lane, London W8 5TZ, England
Penguin Putnam Inc., 375 Hudson Street, New York, New York 10014, USA
Penguin Books Australia Ltd, Ringwood, Victoria, Australia
Penguin Books Canada Ltd, 10 Alcorn Avenue, Toronto, Ontario, Canada M4V 3B2
Penguin Books (NZ) Ltd, Private Bag 102902, NSMC, Auckland, New Zealand

Penguin Books Ltd, Registered Offices: Harmondsworth, Middlesex, England

First published by Victor Gollancz Ltd, 1980
Published in Puffin Books 1982
This edition with new illustrations published in Puffin Books 1999
1 3 5 7 9 10 8 6 4 2

Text copyright © Dick King-Smith, 1980
Illustrations copyright © Mike Terry, 1999
All rights reserved

Typeset in Baskerville

Made and printed in England by Clays Ltd, St Ives plc

British Library Cataloguing in Publication Data
A CIP catalogue record for this book is available from the British Library

ISBN 0-141-30247-X

Contents

CHAPTER 1

TAKEN AWAY

'Oh, no!' cried Mrs Barleylove miserably. 'Oh no!'

'What is it, my dear?' came the voice of Mrs Gobblespud next door. 'One dead?'

'No,' said Mrs Barleylove. 'Not yet anyway.'

Mrs Barleylove was a pedigree Gloucester Old Spots, a flop-eared white pig spotted with a number of roundish black blobs of colour, as though a giant had flicked his paint-brush at her. During the night she had given birth to eight babies, seven of them all of a size, round and strong-looking and already plumped out with their first milk. But the eighth, she now saw, was a poor spindly little creature, half as big as the rest, with a head too large for its scrawny

body and a look of hopelessness on its face.

It was a runt, a piglet born for some reason far smaller and weaker than its brothers and sisters. In different parts of England they are called by different names – cads, wasters, or nesslegraffs. In Gloucestershire they call them dags.

There was a rustling and a scrabbling in the next sty, and Mrs Gobblespud's head appeared over the wall.

'Oh dearie me,' she said. 'Oh dearie me, Mrs B. Oh, I am sorry. 'Tisn't just a smallish one, is it?'

'No,' said Mrs Barleylove. ''Tis a proper dag.'

Now most of the Old Spots sows in the range of nine sties had probably had a dag at some time in their careers as mothers. It wasn't thought of as a disgrace, something to be whispered about, because it didn't seem to be anyone's fault. But it was thought to be a pity, a great pity, for every sow's ambition was to rear a fine litter of healthy evenly matched youngsters; and as the news spread that morning, there was much worried grunting and rolling of eyes and shaking of long droopy ears.

The servant wouldn't like it either, they said to each other. They thought of the pigman as a servant since he did nothing but minister to their wants; he fed them, he watered them, he cleaned them out and brought them fresh bedding. When the showing season came round, it was his duty to brush and comb and oil those taking part, to bring them to the peak of plump beauty. They spoke of him – and to him, though he could not understand this – simply as 'Pigman', as a Roman noble might have said 'Slave'. Pigman wouldn't be pleased about Mrs Barleylove's dag, for dags, if they survived, grew very very slowly, and were more trouble than they were worth.

Mrs Barleylove's neighbour on the other side was called Mrs Swiller and she was leaning over her wall, gossiping with the next lady down the line, Mrs Swedechopper.

''Tain't just that it's a dag, Mrs Swedechopper,' she said sadly. 'From what I can see of the poor little soul, it's deformed.'

'Deformed, Mrs Swiller?' said Mrs Swede-chopper in a tone of horror. 'Why, whatever do you mean?'

'Well, its front feet ain't right.'

'Not right?'

'No. They do turn inwards. And they don't look like pigs' trotters. More like dogs' feet.'

Mrs Gobblespud too had noticed this further piece of misfortune for poor Mrs Barleylove, and had told her neighbour, Mrs Maizemunch; and everywhere heads were sticking up as the sows rested their forefeet comfortably upon their boundary walls and discussed the situation. Only at Number Five, in the centre of the row of sties, was no head raised, for Mrs Barleylove still stood sadly contemplating her misshapen child, while its seven brothers and sisters squeaked greedily around her legs, begging her to lie down and give them more milk. When she did so, the dag was knocked down in the general rush, and lay for a moment upside down in the straw, his curious clubfeet waving helplessly.

Even when he righted himself and tried to feed, he was continually pushed aside by the others and got very little. From Mrs Troughlicker at Number One to Mrs Grubguzzle at Number Nine everybody was convinced of one thing. Pigman would never let this one stay.

'Pigman'll 'ave 'e,' they said.

'No doubt about it.'

'Stands to reason – with feet like that.'

'Poor little mite.'

'Pigman'll take un away, for sure.' And gloom hung over the pigsties like a black cloud.

The sows never quite knew what happened to a dag, or for that matter a piglet badly hurt by being stepped or lain on by its mother. They knew that the servant came and removed such an unfortunate, so they simply spoke of it as being 'taken away'; they were unaware of the hardwood club which the pigman kept in his meal-shed to deal out merciful death to the weak and the wounded.

Before long, the distant clank of buckets and good

smells blowing on the wind told them that the servant was bringing breakfast and the low grunts of concern changed to loud impatient yells as the dag was forgotten in the excitement of feeding time.

'Hurry up, Pigman!' shouted the sows.

'Stir your stumps, you lazy article!'

'Fair starved, I am!'

''E'm too slow to catch a cold!'

And Mrs Troughlicker at Number One, who would be the first fed, champed her jaws with a noise like clapping hands, and great dribbles of spit ran out of her mouth.

When the pigman had completed his duties and Mrs Grubguzzle's head was deep in the trough at Number Nine, he returned to Mrs Barleylove. Earlier that morning he had seen that the birth was finished and all seemed well, but he had not yet examined the litter. Of course he immediately saw the dag and without hesitation picked it gently up and popped it into the deep pocket of his old coat, unnoticed by the sow busy at her breakfast. Had he wanted to examine or remove a healthy piglet, he would have clamped its mouth shut to prevent its squeals bringing the mother rushing to its defence; but this one, he thought, hadn't the strength for even a squeak.

In the meal-shed he looked more closely at it. In all his long experience he had never seen a piglet with such funny forefeet. The little 'clicks' or points of the tiny hooves were turned inward towards one another, so that the shape of the foot was not sharp but rounded, as Mrs Swiller had said, like a puppy's.

Now Gloucester Old Spots are a rare breed of pig, and the pigman occasionally gave in to the temptation to spare the life of a dag if it was a female. A little sow-piglet, or 'hilt' as he called it, just might grow, even if very slowly, to make a breeding sow one day. But little boar-piglets, called hogs, he wanted nothing to do with if they were born weakly.

Not only was this one a hog. It also had those awful feet. Hanging upon a rusty nail was his hardwood club, and the pigman reached up for it.

CHAPTER 2

NOT 'IT' BUT 'HE'

Strangely enough, people who keep pigs very often seem to look like them. The Pigman was a huge fat person, with short legs and a big stomach. His face had several chins, a squashed nose, and little dark glinty eyes. He also had enormous hands, and in one of these he held the dag as one might hold a bunch of flowers, its bony sad-looking head and curious forefeet sticking out above his curled fingers. He shifted his grasp to hold the creature by its hindlegs, its head now hanging down, and took a good grip on his club with the other hand. At that very moment, he heard a scuttling noise at the other end of the shed, and, turning, he saw a rat running across the top of one of his meal bins.

Now if there was one thing the pigman hated, it was a rat. Rats, as far as he was concerned, were worthless greedy cunning thieves, plotting from dawn to dusk to steal the food of his beloved pigs, and the sight of a rat was enough to make him forget everything else. He dropped the dag head first upon the floor and lumbered towards the meal bin, grunting with fury.

The first thing the dag saw, when it had picked itself up, was bright sunlight outside the door; and it tottered towards it and fell down the concrete steps into the yard. Once outside, it heard in the distance the contented noises of full-fed sows and the squeals of piglets fighting for a place at the milk-bar, and it turned that way. It was weak and confused and hungry and unhappy. But it was also determined, and wanted its mother and was going to find her even if, as seemed likely, it killed it.

It plodded on on its dogfeet and eventually reached the door of Number One, where it had just enough strength left for some feeble squeaking. Mrs Troughlicker's head appeared over the door.

''Pon my soul!' she cried. ''Tis that little dag that Pigman took away! Mrs Barleylove! Mrs Barleylove! 'Tis thy dag! 'Tis little Daggie Dogfoot!'

There was uproar along the row as every sow lurched to her feet, those with piglets shaking them off and scattering them in screaming confusion. Soon upon every front door there rested a pair of trotters, and above each a large drop-eared face gazed down at the object outside Mrs Troughlicker's sty.

Above the hubbub came the deep urgent grunting of little Daggie Dogfoot's mother at Number Five. When Mrs Barleylove had finished breakfast, she had nosed her newborn litter and, though she could not count, had found them all fat and level and had known that Pigman had taken one away. Now, by some miracle, here he was again, not a dozen yards from home.

'Daggie!' she called, 'Daggie! Come on, my son! Don't give up now.'

Slowly the exhausted baby began to cover the last lap, wobbling along past Mrs Boltapple at Number Two, then Mrs Swedechopper, then Mrs Swiller, till at last it stood swaying with weariness at the door of Number Five.

'Mammie,' said Daggie Dogfoot. 'I'm tired. And I'm hungry. Let me in.'

Mrs Barleylove would have broken down the door without a second thought had she been able to, but it was stout, and opened inwards. Rooting frantically at the bottom of it in a vain attempt to lift it off its hinges, she discovered that there was a narrow gap between its lower edge and the concrete, a gap not wide enough to get her snout through or to allow a fat piglet out, but just sufficient perhaps to let a very thin piglet in. She scraped away all the straw from it and snorted madly under it as though she were trying to sniff Daggie in like a vacuum cleaner.

'Come on, my baby,' she said. 'Only just get your head through, and the rest'll follow easy.'

'Go on, littlun!' shouted Mrs Grubguzzle at Number Nine, and she was echoed by Mrs Grazegrass, Mrs Maizemunch, and Mrs Gobblespud, as well as by the ladies whose doors Daggie had already passed.

'Go on, love!' they shouted. 'We'm all behind you!'

And before the combination of their support and his mother's urging and his own determination, with a last desperate effort Daggie Dogfoot somehow squeezed his head beneath the door and scrabbled with his funny forefeet and pushed with his skinny hindlegs and found himself at last back home. He lay exhausted while with tender grunts his mother carefully licked him all over. All down the line there rose up a chorus of snorts of relief, and Mrs Swiller and Mrs Gobblespud got off their doors and up on to their boundary walls for final words of congratulation.

'Love it!' cried Mrs Gobblespud. 'What a brave little pig it is!'

Mrs Barleylove looked up from her licking.

'Begging yer pardon, Mrs Gobblespud,' she said slowly and severely, "'tisn't an "it". He's a "he".'

'She's right,' said Mrs Swiller. 'And not just a "he". I do reckon he's a hero.' And with a few last good wishes both ladies returned to their duties.

Fortunately, by the time Daggie had made his way back to the pigsties, his mother had not only finished her own breakfast but had also given his brothers and sisters theirs. Now therefore she was able to push and prod and nose their well-fed little bodies into the inner covered part of Number Five, to barricade the opening with her great spotted back, and to offer the whole range of the milk-bar to one thin tired little body.

And how he drank! Moving along the line, scrabbling at his mother's side with his puppy's feet, he drank and drank and drank. And as he drank, so colour seemed to come into his skin, and his tummy blew out like a drum, and some sparkle crept into his dull eyes. Ten minutes later, when the pigman looked over the door, he found it hard to recognize his late intended victim.

The pigman's pursuit of the rat had led to much moving of bins and sacks, which in turn had exposed other rats. And from this followed much swearing and heavy breathing and wild swiping with the hardwood club, and cries of 'Dratyer!' and 'Dangyer!' and 'Blastyer!' At the end of it all he was

hot and sweaty, and the rats were laughing in their
runways, and quite a lot of time had passed.

He looked about the doorway end of the meal-
shed, expecting to find the dag hiding somewhere,
then searched the yard, and finally, seeing no sign of
it, walked down to the sties in case it could by any
chance have found its way home. He leaned on the
door of Number Five and shook his head till his
three chins wobbled.

'Never credit it,' he said to himself, mopping his
face with a red spotted handkerchief, 'little chap's got
some guts. But all the same he'll never be no use to
no one, nohow. He'll 'ave to go,' and he slid back the
bolt.

Now Mrs Barleylove busy at breakfast and unaware of the fact – though resigned to the possibility – that one of her children was to be taken away was one thing. Mrs Barleylove interrupted while feeding that hero of a child was another; interrupted moreover by an impudent servant who had no right in her house except at feeding or cleaning-out times, and who was clearly intending to try to take her baby away once more.

Heaving herself to her feet with a violence that threw a surprised Daggie far to one side, she ran at the servant, swinging her head and champing her jaws together so that a froth of bubbles ran out over her tusks. The champing and her furious grunting combined to make a noise that sounded to the pigman like 'Out! Out! Out!' which in fact was exactly what she was saying. At the same time, Mrs Swiller and Mrs Gobblespud reared up on to their walls and also shouted angrily at the servant.

'You leave 'im alone, Pigman!' they roared.

'Poor little feller.'

'Tackle somebody your own size!'

'Dirty fat man!'

For just as we say 'dirty as a pig' or 'fat as a pig', so pigs repay the insult the other way round. And all along the row, from Mrs Troughlicker to Mrs Grubguzzle the cry went up 'Dirty fat man! Let un alone! Get off out of it!' while nine pairs of jaws champed and nine pairs of eyes glistened.

The pigman was indeed out of Number Five remarkably quickly for a man of his size. He knew all about the damage an angry sow can cause, and it was a different kind of sweat which he now wiped from his brow.

'Dratyer!' he cried, and 'Dangyer!' and 'Blastyer!'

He waited until the fuming Mrs Barleylove had got down off the top of her door, and then bolted it, and lumbered off grumbling to himself. Let her keep the 'orrible little dag, he thought, it'll die soon enough and save me the trouble. Cussed old sows!

And as men often do when they feel that womenfolk are too much for them, he walked across the yard to seek the company of another male, for the Gloucester Old Spots boar lived opposite. The boar came to his door, and gave his usual order.

'Hey you, Pigman. Scratch my back.' And the servant of course obeyed. 'He's not a bad chap really,' thought the boar. 'Does what he's told.'

'Now he's a good old chap,' thought the pigman. 'Aren't you, old man?' he said. 'Not like they cussed old sows.'

And indeed, excepting that one was spotted and one was not, they looked very alike as they stood and chatted, each in his own tongue.

CHAPTER 3

Pigs Might Fly

Time passed, and Daggie Dogfoot not only survived but grew. He did not expand visibly like his litter-mates, but by cunning and agility he secured a fair share of his mother's milk. For example, he would persuade her to lie across a corner in which he was already waiting, or stand alongside the concrete feeding-trough so that he could scramble on to its rim for a high-level drink which the others couldn't reach; their slippery sharp-hooved forefeet did not allow them to balance there.

The pigman became resigned to Daggie's survival, and persuaded himself he had kept the creature out of kindness, as a mascot. Well aware of the look in

Mrs Barleylove's eye and the sound of her threatening grunts, he left the dag severely alone.

Mrs Barleylove's neighbours spent a lot of their spare time leaning over their respective walls to watch. Unlike the pigman, who was merely pretending as an excuse, they really did regard Daggie as a mascot, as indeed did all the other mothers; no piglet before had ever been 'taken away' and then come back, and there seemed something magical, mystical almost, about this, and also about his feet which appeared at the moment to be an advantage to him rather than the reverse.

'Love him!' said Mrs Gobblespud one morning, after watching Daggie do his king-of-the-castle trick on the trough. 'He's growed ever so smart, an't 'e, Mrs B?'

Mrs Barleylove only grunted but inwardly she swelled with pride. She had never believed in having favourites among her many children, but she had to admit to herself that this one was very . . . special.

'No offence,' said Mrs Swiller, 'but his little feet have altered, an't they?' And indeed, though the hooves on Daggie's hindfeet remained normal, the grotesquely inward-curving horny parts on his front feet had fallen off, leaving even more puppy-like round pads. This seemed to make him more surefooted, so that when the litter played a game of tag, racing round the smooth clean-washed concrete of the outer enclosure after Pigman had mucked out, it was always Daggie who kept his feet while his stronger brothers and sisters often slipped and skidded on to their sides.

Mrs Barleylove was half minded to take offence at such a personal remark, but she quickly realized that it was well-meant; and anyway she badly wanted her neighbours' opinions.

'Yes, he has growed. And they have altered,' she said. 'Tell you the truth, ladies, I'd be mortal glad to know what you do think. You might say I'm daft, but I've caught meself wondering if he ain't somehow . . .' she paused and looked round to make sure that Daggie was not listening but he had run off with the

rest for a rough-and-tumble in the straw inside, so she went on '. . . somehow . . . special?'

'Special?' said Mrs Swiller.

'Well, born for some purpose.'

'Purpose?' said Mrs Gobblespud.

'What I mean to say is,' said Mrs Barleylove, 'he was taken away, wasn't he?'

'Must-a been,' they said.

'And yet he come back?'

'For certain sure,' they said.

'So that's kind of . . . special?'

Long droopy ears slap-slapped against fat faces as the two ladies nodded vigorous agreement.

'And his front feet?' said Mrs Barleylove.

'Different,' said Mrs Swiller.

'Curious,' said Mrs Gobblespud.

'Special?' asked Mrs Barleylove. There was a pause.

'Do you mean,' said her neighbours, 'special feet . . . for some purpose?'

It was Mrs Barleylove's turn to nod. There was another pause, during which the neighbours glanced a little anxiously at each other over her head. It occurred to them simultaneously that this was going a bit too far. Mrs Barleylove's concern for her dag was leading her to flights of fancy. Special feet for some purpose? No, no, that was too much of a good thing.

'Well . . . no, dear, not really,' said Mrs Gobblespud in a kindly voice, 'I mean, I know they're not like other piglets' front feet are, but . . .'

'What Mrs G means, dear,' said Mrs Swiller soothingly, 'is that you shouldn't worry yourself overly about the little chap's feet. I mean I don't personally think they're going to be a hindrance to him, quite the contrary, but as to having been made like that for some purpose, well, that's about as likely as that . . .'

'. . . pigs might fly,' finished Mrs Gobblespud.

As Mrs Swiller had hesitated, Daggie Dogfoot had been on the point of coming out from the inner part of the sty, impelled as children often are by the certain feeling that adults are talking about them. All he heard in fact were the last three words. What's more, his mother and her friends fell silent the moment they saw him, so he felt sure he had been right.

'Good morning, Auntie Swiller, good morning, Auntie Gobblespud,' he said politely. And then, 'Can I have a milk shake, please, Mammie – quick, before the others come back?'

The sows' conversation thus abruptly terminated, the neighbours dropped back off their walls, and Mrs Barleylove lay hastily down, anxious to please her darling.

Even as he gollupped down milk, Daggie was

thinking hard. Pigs might fly, he thought, and they were definitely talking about me; that must mean I might fly. The other piglets came dashing out at that moment, and scrambled and shoved and stamped all over him, but he hung on determinedly until he was finished, and then climbed up and lay down on the huge rubbery cushion of his mother's side.

He looked at his curious feet about which the others already teased him, though he did not mind for he was glad to be alive. He looked up at the blue sky. A sparrow flew over the sty with a whirr of wings; a little higher, a flock of starlings made their way across the yard; higher still, the swallows and martins cut lovely circles in the fly-filled air and

above them all, so high that his baby eyes could barely see them, the swifts raced black and crescent-shaped, screaming their joy at the wonder of flight.

I . . . might fly, thought Daggie Dogfoot. He sat up on his mother and beat his forelegs together experimentally, but nothing happened. Perhaps it's taking off that's difficult, he thought. Perhaps once you get up there, it's easier. He looked up into the sky again and tried to imagine himself up there, legs beating away somehow or other, ears flapping, curly tail stretched out straight behind him as he soared and glided and swooped.

Perhaps if I got up somewhere high, he thought, so that I could jump off and then start flying. I'm sure they were talking about me. I'm sure I could do it. I will do it, you see if I don't. Just give me half a chance.

CHAPTER 4

THE SQUIRE

The boar was of course the most important person around, partly because he was an incredibly well-bred and aristocratic Gloucester Old Spots, and partly because he was the father of all the children born. His real name was Champion Imperial Challenger III of Ploughbarrow, but the sows all knew him as the Squire. His sty, which was opposite the row of nine, had a sloping verandah-type roof to keep the rain off his noble back, and the pigman, being large, had to duck down under this whenever he went in; the sows appreciated the fact that the servant always bowed low before the master.

The Squire kept in touch with his wives by means of occasional conversations across the yard when he felt like it and the wind was not too strong. He would stand against his door and poke his head out under his verandah roof and shout at them in his bluff jolly way. Sometimes he would address them generally, and then everyone who was not actually engaged at that moment in feeding babies would come respectfully to their front doors and bob their heads up and down deferentially. Sometimes he would single out an individual, to enquire after the latest arrivals perhaps.

One morning some weeks after Daggie Dogfoot's birth, his deep coughing grunt was heard, and the rattle of his door as he heaved his bulk up on to it. ''Tis the Squire!' they all said to their neighbours, and waited in awestruck silence. The boar cleared his throat.

'Ah, hhhrm, Mrs Barleylove, dear lady. A word with you.'

'Here I be, Squire,' said Mrs Barleylove. 'What was you wanting?'

'The latest children, my dear. I hear from sparrow-talk that you have a litter?' The sparrows carried all the gossip round the farm.

'Y-yes, Squire.'

'All well, I trust? Bonny? Bouncing? Chips off the old block, what?' There was a moment's pause and a shudder of anticipation ran down the sties. But Mrs Barleylove was equal to the occasion.

'All well, I thank you, Squire,' she replied, with hardly a tremor in her voice. 'Thanking yer honour for your kindness in enquiring.'

'Good show,' said the Squire. 'Fine effort, doncherknow. Keep up the good work, what?' and he got down off his door, while all the ladies ducked their heads again and disappeared with a whistling sound which was made up of eight small sighs of relief and one large one.

It was not that the Squire didn't know about dags. He knew only too well, because a litter-sister of his had been one. He had never forgotten waking up one morning when he was a baby, to find the poor spindly little thing stretched out cold and lifeless beside him; and because of this he was always terrified that one of his own children might be born a dag.

So he always asked the same question, 'Chips off the old block, what?', and the sows never let him down. He never knew that occcasionally the chips were very small, and either died or were taken away; and as for the occasional hilt whose life the pigman saw fit to spare, the Squire would not set eyes on it until it was weaned and on its way to other quarters. If it survived that long, it would have caught up a bit in size and be nothing worse than the smallest of the litter. But what on earth would he say to Daggie Dogfoot?

Mrs Barleylove's neighbours tried to find a tactful way to approach the subject. They began with praise.

'Ain't he active?' said Mrs Gobblespud admiringly as she watched Daggie, his mind on flight, leap from his mother's back and land upside down in the remains of breakfast at the bottom of the trough. 'You must be proud of him, Mrs B.'

'Any mother would be proud of him,' said Mrs Swiller. And then, greatly daring, she added defiantly, 'And any father too.'

There was a long awkward pause, and it seemed

to the neighbours that Mrs Barleylove's white parts grew a little pink and her spots turned slightly blacker.

'I don't rightly know what to do, ladies,' she said at last. 'Squire's bound to clap eyes on him sooner or later. He'll go raving mad.'

''Tis more sooner than later though, ain't it?' said Mrs Gobblespud. 'They'll be crossing the yard in a week or so, won't 'em?'

'Crossing the yard' meant weaning time, when the eight-week-old piglets left their mothers and went to the store pens on either side of the boar's sty; later the hogs would go to the fattening pens, and the hilts to other quarters till big enough to be sold for breeding.

Daggie, though he had not been listening to the conversation properly, had, like children everywhere, picked up the awkward bits.

'Who's Squire, Mammie?' he asked.

'The Squire is your father, dear, a very fine gentleman.'

'Why will he go raving mad?'

'Oh, your father's a hot-tempered person,' said Mrs Swiller quickly. 'He gets very angry with the servant if his meals are late.'

'Well, what's "crossing the yard" mean, Auntie Swiller?'

'Oh, you'll like that, Daggie,' put in Mrs

Gobblespud soothingly. 'That's when all the young 'uns go off on a lovely holiday and your mother gets a nice rest.'

Mrs Barleylove's other seven piglets jumped about excitedly at this, and ran about the sty squealing 'A lovely holiday! A lovely holiday!' But Daggie Dogfoot sat on his thin backside, and a tear ran down the side of his big head.

'I don't want to leave my Mammie,' he said, and another tear ran down the other side.

At that moment Mrs Barleylove made up her mind, quite firmly, that she would not allow this humble undersized deformed child of hers to cross the yard. Always before, like all the other mothers, she had allowed the servant to drive the weaners away without protest, indeed with a sigh of relief after two months' hard work. This time it would be different, for this child was different, and her heart ached at the sight of those two great tears. The servant could take the other seven, but not her Daggie. Just let him try.

A fortnight later he tried. He opened the door of Number Five, and holding a sheet of corrugated iron in front of him like a shield, he hooshed Mrs Barleylove into the inner part of the sty while the litter ran out into the yard. A grunt and a rattle on the other side told everyone that the Squire was at his door to inspect his offspring as they crossed. But when the pigman had shut up Number Five again, he could only count seven fat weaners frisking about outside. He looked back in and saw the dag peeping out from between his mother's legs. He started to open the door again but immediately Mrs Barleylove rushed forward, champing and snorting, fierce as one of her wild woodland ancestors.

'Dirty fat man!' she shouted. 'Let un alone!'

'Dratyer!' cried the pigman, and 'Dangyer!' and 'Blastyer!'

But he backed away quickly, and then turned and lumbered off after the rest.

'Keep the mizzable thing then!' he shouted back over his shoulder. ''Twill never be no use to no one, nohow!'

He rounded up the others, drove them into a V-shaped funnel of hurdles which he had put up, and so into one of the store pens, and shut them in. He mopped his face with his red spotted handkerchief and went to talk to Champion Imperial Challenger III of Ploughbarrow.

'Hey you, Pigman. Scratch my back,' said the Squire. And, as usual, the servant obeyed. They held a conversation, and it was fortunate that they spoke different languages.

'Damn fine bunch of youngsters that, Pigman,' said the Squire, 'fat as you are by the time they're finished, I shouldn't wonder.'

'You got an 'orrible little dag left over there, old feller,' said the pigman. 'That bad-tempered old sow's welcome to him.'

And what a welcome Daggie Dogfoot was having, for his mother still had plenty of milk left for one, and now the whole milk-bar was his and his alone.

At last, full to the brim, he fell asleep by his mother's side, and dreamed that he and she and his father the Squire were all flying, trotter in trotter, through a warm and milky sky.

CHAPTER 5

Resthaven

The sows usually had two litters of babies each year, in the Spring and in the Autumn; and so twice a year, after weaning her piglets, every mother enjoyed what Mrs Gobblespud had called 'a good rest'. As soon as a newly weaned litter had 'crossed the yard', the sow would expect the servant to open her door and then a gate at the upper end of the cluster of farm buildings. This gate was the entrance to a small field which the pigman unimaginatively called 'the Pig Ground', but to which the ladies always referred as 'Resthaven'.

'Not long now,' a harassed mother would say to her neighbour at about the seventh week of nursing. 'Soon be going to Resthaven.'

'Oh, that'll be nice for you, dear.'

'Lovely and quiet there.'

'The air's good too. So bracing.'

'Not but what I shan't miss the kiddies, mind.'

'No, but you got to get away. Besides, it gives that lazy Pigman time to give the house a good clean-up.'

Resthaven was a small triangular patch of roughish hillside, sloping down from a point at the top to a long base bounded by a brook. The other two sides were fenced with stout pig-wire, and right in the centre stood a great old oak. Most of the upper part of the little field was dotted with ant heaps.

The morning after Daggie's brothers and sisters had left, the pigman came to Number Five and opened the door. Normally on these occasions one or two heads might pop up along the row, and one or two shouts be heard of 'Have a nice time!' or 'Happy holidays!' But this time it was different, for no one remembered a piglet ever going to Resthaven, much less a dag. By the time Daggie had politely said goodbye to Auntie Swiller and Auntie Gobblespud, every other head was up to see this strange baby. And as Mrs Barleylove made her stately way off after the lumbering servant, with Daggie trotting behind her, many and heartfelt were the good wishes that followed them, though softly spoken so as not to wake the Squire.

For Daggie, everything was new and wonderful. No sooner had the servant closed the gate than the little piglet cried, 'Oh, Mammie! Isn't it exciting? Can I go off and explore?'

'Go where you like, my love,' said his mother. 'But mind and be careful of the water at the bottom of the field. Pigs can't swim, you know.'

Pigs might fly though, thought Daggie Dogfoot gleefully to himself as he ran away over the summer grasses. Specially if they could find somewhere high enough to jump off.

Mrs Barleylove, watching her darling with pride, was quite amazed to see how fast he made his way around Resthaven, scampering down to the brook to peer at the glistening tinkling water, rushing up through patches of reed and coarse grass to scratch himself against the rough trunk of the oak, and skipping on and off the ant heaps more like a lamb than a piglet. Doggy little forefeet and skinny long hindlegs he might have, but he was quicker and more active, she thought, than any of the dozens of fat rolypoly babies she had had in her long life of motherhood.

Finally, as she watched, Daggie arrived at the very top of the wedge-shaped field and climbed upon the highest of all the ant heaps. He turned to face downhill and saw his mother looking up towards him. 'Watch me, Mammie!' he yelled, and leaped off.

He nosedived into the grass, turned a somersault, rolled over a couple of times on the steep slope, and fetched up against the next ant heap six feet away.

'Yes, dear. Very clever,' called Mrs Barleylove tenderly, and went to the oak to look for acorns.

By the end of that first thrilling day Daggie was pretty sore. He had climbed on to and jumped off everything he could find, every bank and ridge in the rough field, every ant heap, and several stumps of felled elms. He had even somehow climbed to the highest part of a big dead branch that lay on the ground beneath the oak, and taken off from a height of perhaps four feet. But every effort had resulted in a crash landing, and now, in the warmth of the August evening, he was not only bruised but a little despondent.

He and his mother had just left a shallow place at the brook's edge where they had drunk their fill, and now they stood together at a point further along the bank, a high point where the stream had cut away the side over the years as it made a swirling turn. Here they were about fifteen feet above the water, and behind them the slope of Resthaven was steep and shortgrassed for some distance.

Suppose I started back up there and ran really fast, thought Daggie. 'Mammie,' he said, 'did you say pigs couldn't swim?'

Mrs Barleylove, like all her kind, had been brought

up to believe the old sows' tale that a pig attempting to swim will cut its own throat by the awkward action of its sharp-hooved forefeet; and she explained this to her son. She was comfortably full of acorns and roots and grasses and berries, as well as the ration of pig-nuts which the servant had brought, and she gazed dreamily down at the winking water without really thinking what she was saying.

'But I haven't got . . .' began Daggie, and then some instinct checked him.

'What, dear?' said Mrs Barleylove absently.

'Er, I haven't heard that before,' said Daggie quickly. 'I mean, I didn't know that.'

'There's lots of things you don't know, my son,'

said his mother in the way that mothers always do.

And there's something that you don't know too, thought the dag to himself. Which is that if I started back up there and ran really fast . . . Pigs *might* fly, he said to himself, Auntie Gobblespud said so. I just wish I had the chance to consult an expert before trying. Daggie had thought a good deal about getting expert advice, and had often asked the birds who hopped around Number Five. But the sparrows, when he questioned them, only answered 'Cheap! Cheap!' in an impudent way, and the starlings simply piped rudely at him; once a big carrion crow had pitched on the sty wall but in reply to the piglet's enquiries only said 'Garn!'

Suddenly, as he stood by his mother high above the brook, there was a whistle of wings and over their heads flew a black-and-white bird with a bright red bill and cheek-patches, and wide webbed feet with sharp claws at the ends of the toes. Beating its wings rapidly, it braked and dropped upon the surface in a shower of waterdrops that gleamed golden in the sunlight. Wagging its tail feathers from side to side, it swam rapidly about, first drinking, and then showering itself with water by splashing with its wings.

Flying *and* swimming, thought Daggie. Too much!

'What's that bird, Mammie?' he asked. 'I've never seen one like that before.'

'There's lots of things you've never seen before, dear,' said his mother in the way that mothers always do. 'That's a duck.'

'Where does it come from?' asked Daggie.

'Oh, Pigman keeps some, I believe,' said Mrs Barleylove. 'For their eggs, I think. After all,' she went on reflectively, 'even servants have to eat, I suppose. Let them eat eggs.'

'Can I talk to it, Mammie?' said Daggie Dogfoot eagerly. 'It won't hurt me, will it?'

'Won't hurt you,' said his mother. 'But I don't suppose you'll get much out of it. They'm stupid things. Probably won't understand a word you say.' But when Daggie ran down to the shallow place and called to the duck, it immediately turned and swam towards him with a pleasant expression on its neat face.

CHAPTER 6

FELICITY

'Good-mor-ning-duck,' said Daggie Dogfoot very slowly and loudly, the proper way to address foreigners, 'can-I-ask-you-some-thing-please?' The duck, which had been walking towards him up the sandy shallows with a quick rolling gait, hopped up on to a low willow branch, gripped it comfortably with her clawed feet, settled her feathers, and considered the piglet with bright eyes.

'Absolutely anything you like,' she answered in a quiet musical voice.

'Oh,' said Daggie, surprised, 'Mammie said you wouldn't . . .' He stopped, confused.

'. . . wouldn't understand a word you said?'

38

chuckled the duck. 'Well, your mother obviously doesn't know much about Muscovy ducks.'

Daggie gulped. 'Please,' he said, 'what is a . . . Muscovy duck?'

'Well,' said the duck, 'we're a tree-perching variety – that's what these are for,' and she raised one foot to show the curved claws. 'Originally from South America.'

Daggie's world had expanded enormously since leaving Number Five, but it was still very small. He imagined South America to be the next field beyond Resthaven.

'Anyway,' said the duck, 'what did you want to ask me?'

Daggie took a deep breath. He looked up at the steep bank above to see if his mother was there, but she had moved away.

'Do you think,' he said slowly and carefully, 'that pigs might fly?' The duck opened her bill wide, and then hastily closed it again. Then she opened and closed it rapidly perhaps a dozen times, making a soft quot-quot-quotting noise.

'Well, do you?' asked Daggie.

'I think,' said the duck, 'that almost anything *might* happen. Though I have never actually heard of a flying pig. Who put the idea in your head?'

'My Auntie,' said Daggie. 'Well, she was our next-door neighbour really but I called her Auntie. She said it, you see, and I'm pretty sure they were all talking about me.'

'So it's you that's going to ... fly?' said the Muscovy.

'Hope so.'

'Have you tried yet?'

'Oh yes, quite a few times. But I can't seem to get airborne. That's why I'm so excited about this place.' And Daggie proceeded to explain to his new friend his idea of the steep downhill take-off and the leap from the top of the high bank into glorious soaring flight. 'D'you think I could do it?' said Daggie Dogfoot.

The bright-eyed duck looked consideringly at this strange creature before her. She looked at his big head and his hard thin little body and his skinny backside. She looked down at the sand and saw the three sets of prints on it, her own webs, the deep slots of the heavy sow, and the third strange set of tracks of two tiny slots and two pawmarks. The idea of a modest lecture on the qualities necessary for flight occurred to her, but she dismissed it immediately in the face of the determination which shone from the piglet's features.

'I think you're going to try,' she said. And looking at the deep pool which the current had gouged out below the steep bank, she added, 'It's not a bad place to try either. I presume you can swim?'

Daggie looked puzzled.

'Pigs can't swim,' he said. 'I should have thought you would have known that. I'm not talking about swimming. I'm talking about flying.'

The duck hopped off the willow branch and walked over to Daggie. Pretending to squatter in the damp sand with her bill, she shot a close look at the piglet's forefeet. I wonder, she thought. His highflown ambitions are going to flop, that's for sure. But something else quite novel might come out of it.

'Tell you what,' she said. 'I'd love to see the . . . er, maiden flight. Would you mind?'

'Not a bit,' replied Daggie excitedly. 'That's exactly what I wanted – an expert to be around to give me tips. I mean it isn't just the take-off. I may need some help with landing.'

Once again the duck made that soft quot-quot-quotting noise with her bill.

'Yes,' she said. 'Though coming down is really the easiest bit. By the way, what does your mother think about all this?'

'Oh, she doesn't know,' said Daggie. 'I thought I'd try it very early in the morning while she's having her lie-in. How about tomorrow?'

'All right,' said the duck. 'I'll be in the pool here at sunrise tomorrow. By the way, I don't know your name?'

'Daggie Dogfoot,' said the piglet.

'Right,' said the duck. She slipped into the water and began to paddle off upstream.

'Wait a minute,' called Daggie after her. 'How will you get here that early? Won't you have to wait till Pigman lets you out?'

The duck stopped paddling and floated back towards him on the current.

'Pigman?' she said.

'Yes, the servant,' said Daggie. 'You know, that dirty fat man.'

'Oh, Duckman you mean,' said the Muscovy. 'Oh no, I don't go in the shed at nights with the rest of them. I roost in a tree.'

You might suppose Duckman just keeps us for the

eggs we lay, she thought, but I've seen him before now go into the shed with an empty sack and come out with it full and kicking. I'm not taking any risks. And off she swam once more. She was almost round the next bend in the stream before Daggie realized he did not know her name. He ran through the shallow water on to the bank and galloped along till he came level with her.

'What are you called?' he shouted down.

'Felicity,' said the duck.

'That's a funny name,' shouted Daggie. 'What's it mean?'

'Happiness,' said the duck, and paddled away past the boundary of Resthaven and out of the piglet's sight.

Happiness, thought Daggie, as he made his way towards his mother who was lying under the oak tree, life seems to be full of it. Living in this lovely place, and making such a nice friend, and tomorrow . . . wheeeee! Mrs Barleylove woke up from her nap at his squealing arrival.

'Where you bin, my baby?' she asked. 'Talking to that duck?' and she grunted with amusement.

'Yes, Mammie,' said Daggie excitedly, 'and she's ever so nice and she's called Felicity and . . .' he took a deep breath '. . . she's a Muscovy from South America.'

'Fancy!' said Mrs Barleylove. 'There's nice.'

What an imagination, she thought fondly. Just sees an old duck in the brook, and he comes out with all that fairy story. Bless his little heart.

'You come and have a nice rest,' she said. 'You don't want to overtire yourself. Tomorrow's another day.'

But as Daggie Dogfoot lay by his mother's side and dozed in the sheltered warmth of Resthaven while the afternoon shadows lengthened, he knew that tomorrow wasn't just another day. Tomorrow was the day he had been planning for ages and ages, a whole two weeks, a quarter of his life. Tomorrow was the day he would fly. And Felicity would be there to help him. His mouth screwed into a grin of pure joy, he fell soundly asleep.

CHAPTER 7

GOSH!

Felicity woke early next morning on her usual perch. This was the thin branch of an alder tree sticking out over the stream. She had chosen it not only because it was completely fox-proof, but because she liked the never-ending music of the running water, singing her to sleep with its bubbling lullaby and waking her each day with its gurgling song.

She stretched her wings, one after the other, pushing out each in its turn to its fullest extent so that the big flight feathers stood apart from each other, as a human might stretch his fingers wide. Then she flapped her wings very vigorously as she stood up on the branch and shook herself all over. She felt very happy.

She began to think about her new friend Daggie Dogfoot. He's in for a ducking, she thought with amusement, and then it suddenly struck her that a ducking might easily turn into a drowning. She jumped off her alder branch and flew rapidly downstream towards Resthaven. She was suddenly worried that the piglet might have been too impatient to wait for her.

However, as soon as she reached the little sloping field she could see that everything was in order. Under the oak lay a mountain of spotted flesh, which was Mrs Barleylove having her lie-in. And at the top of the steep slope above the high bank, a small spotty figure positively danced with impatience, pawing at the ground with his round front feet as though he were a puppy on an invisible leash.

'Hello, Felicity!' cried Daggie as the duck glided over his head. 'Take-off in two minutes. OK?'

A minute and three-quarters later the first rays of the rising sun came over the eastern bank of Resthaven and shone upon the rough bark of the oak tree and upon the smooth, closed, white-lashed eyelids of Mrs Barleylove. She opened her eyes, stretched, heaved herself to her feet, and looked about for her beloved boy. Hardly had she focused upon him, high above her on the slope, than to her absolute horror she saw him begin to run downhill at great speed, faster, faster, faster, till at last he leaped out over the high bank of the stream, and disappeared from her sight.

Felicity had positioned herself close under the Resthaven bank of the brook, directly underneath the take-off point. She knew that the impetus of his downhill run would take Daggie well out into the middle of the pool, and, head cocked upwards, she waited, ready to go instantly to his aid.

Suddenly the quiet of the morning was shattered by an anguished scream from the horrified watcher under the oak tree, and in the same instant, high above the waiting duck, a small spotted shape shot out from the top of the bank and seemed for a frozen fraction of time to hang suspended against the clear blue sky. Legs working frantically, ears streaming behind his head, ridiculous tail whipping round and round like an egg-whisk, Daggie Dogfoot enjoyed a split second of level flight. Then his heavy head came down to point him at the pool, a squeal of fright burst from him as the dark water rushed up to greet him, and 'Eeeeeeek – kersplosh – glug!' he was gone from view.

When he rose to the surface, he was facing the opposite bank and could not see the reassuring figure of the Muscovy duck, who had by now swum close to him. He could see nothing but what seemed an ocean of water of which he had already swallowed a lot, and on top of the newfound knowledge that pigs couldn't fly came the awful realization that they couldn't swim either. He knew this. Mammie had said so. Mammie, whom he would never see again.

'Heeeelp!' he squealed. 'Heee-gurgle-glug!' and down he went again. As soon as he surfaced for the second time he heard two voices. One was his mother's, shouting desperately from the shallows where she stood belly-deep after a thundering gallop from the oak tree.

'Save him! Save my boy!' yelled Mrs Barleylove in agony.

The other was a quiet voice which spoke in his ear.

'Keep still,' said the quiet voice. 'Don't struggle. Don't talk. Keep your mouth tight shut. Breathe through your snout. Run after me. Just run as though you were on dry land,' and Felicity set off for the far bank which was by now the nearer of the two, wagging her tail encouragingly and glancing back over her shoulder at the piglet.

Because of the confidence in the duck's voice, because he had spirit and courage still in the midst of his panic, and because there was nothing else to do, Daggie obeyed. He clenched his teeth together, tipped up his head so that his nostrils pointed skywards like the twin guns of a surfaced submarine, kicked with his hindlegs and paddled like mad with his doggy feet, trying hard to imagine that he was galloping through the grass.

To his amazement, he began to move forward through the water after the duck, at first slowly, then faster as he gained momentum and confidence, and finally so fast that before they reached the far bank he was level with her and they touched bottom together in a little reedy inlet.

They looked at one another and their eyes shone, Felicity's with amusement and pleasure, Daggie's with relief and triumph as realization swept over him.

'Pigs can't fly,' said Daggie. Felicity shook her head.

'But there's one pig,' said Daggie quietly, 'that can,' said Daggie more loudly, 'SWIM!' shouted Daggie Dogfoot at the top of his squeaky voice, and off he set, all by himself, towards his mother on the Resthaven bank.

Mrs Barleylove had continued throughout to yell 'Save my boy!' pausing only when it seemed he had reached safety. Now here he was back in deep water again, and she began to squeal as before, until two voices reached her ears.

'Calm yourself, missus,' said one as the duck, who had flown quickly across over the head of the swimmer, landed beside her. 'He's all right. Just listen to him.' And as the sow quietened, she heard the other voice, the voice of her fast-approaching son.

'Mammie! Mammie!' came the cry over the gentle lapping of the pool. 'Look at me! I can swim! It's easy! Watch!' and as she stared, open-mouthed, the small figure came paddling nearer and nearer, pushing up a little bow wave in front of it with the speed of its progress.

Still Mrs Barleylove did not really understand what had happened since the sun had woken her. As soon as Daggie was out of the brook and shaking himself like a water-spaniel, she turned and made off up the bank towards the summit, scolding as she went in the way that mothers do when their children have given them a bad fright.

'Silly boy!' she said. 'Naughty boy! Come quickly and run about in the sunshine or you'll catch your death of cold. I told you not to go down by the water. You'm never to go there again, d'you understand? Never. I don't know what your father would say if he knew,' and so on, until, receiving no reply, she turned and found that she had been talking to herself.

Below her, as she stood at the take-off point on the top of the high bank, two figures swam happily about the pool. One was white with black patches, and one was white with black spots, and as Mrs Barleylove watched giddily from the height they made a series of patterns in the pool, first one leading, then the other. Circles they made, and figures-of-eight, and zigzags, and criss-crosses, till the surface frothed and little wavelets lapped and slapped against the banks.

Slowly the incredible truth dawned upon Mrs Barleylove. Her poor undersized deformed child was swimming, really swimming, swimming beautifully. 'Special feet for some purpose', eh? If only the neighbours could see him now.

'Oh, Daggie my love!' she called down. 'How clever you be!'

How happy I am, thought Daggie, to have such a lovely mother, to swim in this beautiful sparkling stuff, to be with my friend whose very name means happiness. And he paddled madly about, while every little fish in the pool formed its mouth into a perfect round o of wonder. The moorhens in the reeds tut-tutted their amazement. The heron on the top of a downstream willow squawked his disbelief. A brilliant kingfisher gave an admiring whistle, and a passing green woodpecker laughed hysterically. And up the line of the brook flew a solitary swan, the sound of his great wings expressing exactly the surprise of all. 'Gosh!' was the noise they made. 'Gosh! Gosh! Gosh! Gosh!'

CHAPTER 8

THE TRUTH
COMES OUT

The news travelled fast, by air mail of course, for the woodpecker shouted it to his mate in her nesting hole, and starlings resting in upper branches heard it; later they discussed it in wheezy whistles as they bathed in the yard trough; sparrows searching the floor for small seeds listened to the starlings, and then of course told everybody. By midday there was only one creature who did not know the story of the swimming piglet, and that of course was the pigman, too stupid to understand animal language. The Squire knew, as the sows soon found out.

Mrs Swiller and Mrs Gobblespud were conversing across the empty outer run of Number Five, now brushed and scraped and washed clean by the servant, and smelling strongly of disinfectant. They were recalling a conversation of a couple of weeks ago.

'Do ee recall what she said, Mrs G?' grunted Mrs Swiller.

'That I do, Mrs S,' replied Mrs Gobblespud, 'that I do. Special, she said. Special feet, that's what she said. And do you remember what we said?'

'That I do, Mrs G,' answered Mrs Swiller. 'Sure as my name's Rosie Swiller, I do. "Special feet for some purpose", that's what we asked if she meant. Rubbish, we thought.'

'Just fancy!' said Mrs Gobblespud. She paused, consideringly.

'Wouldn't cut his throat, see,' she went on.

'Not with feet like that,' said Mrs Swiller.

'Always said he were a clever little chap.'

'And brave with it.'

'Never heard of any Ploughbarrow pig swimming, never.'

'Never heard of any pig swimming.'

'What'll Pigman say when he finds out?'

There was a short silence, and then with one horrified voice they said, 'What'll Squire say when he finds out?'

The words were hardly out of their mouths when they heard the deep grunt and the rattle of the door on the other side of the yard. Mrs Swiller and Mrs Gobblespud slid back off their walls and stood very still in their sties, heads lowered, breath held. If they had had fingers, they would have crossed them. Neither wanted in the least to hear her name called if the boar started asking questions. As it turned out, no one was to escape.

'Ladies!' barked the Squire in his loudest voice. 'A word with you all, if ye please. My apologies if any of you are in the midst of your duties, but I want you all on parade in one minute.'

At these stern words there was a tremendous noise of hustling and bustling and shuffling mixed with the squeals of rudely disturbed piglets, and within thirty seconds eight pairs of trotters reared up on to eight front doors, and above them eight large anxious faces peered across at the lord and master.

Only at Number Five of course was there no face, and it seemed to the nervous sows that the Squire's angry gaze was directed at this space rather than at any one of them. After a moment however he shifted his look to Number One, and then slowly, deliberately, swung his heavy head to scrutinize in turn each face, all the way to Number Nine.

At last he spoke. 'It has come to my notice,' he said, 'that something very strange has been going on, doncherknow. What?'

No one answered, so he went on, 'Now I'm going to get to the bottom of this, dammit, so I shall ask you all in turn. And I don't want any shilly-shallying, what? Understood?'

'Yes, Squire,' chorused eight worried voices.

The Squire looked directly at Number One again. 'Mrs Troughlicker,' he said. 'The damned sparrows are talking about a swimming pig. What d'ye know about it, eh?'

'Not a great deal, Squire,' said Mrs Troughlicker uncomfortably, 'there's rumours.'

'Mrs Boltapple?'

'Don't hardly seem possible, Squire.'

'Mrs Swedechopper?'

'Well, Squire, perhaps somebody was mistook.'

'Mrs Swiller?'

Mrs Swiller hesitated, and glanced nervously across at Mrs Gobblespud.

'Well, Mrs Swiller?'

'Tidn't one of mine, Squire, they'm all here, dry as a bone, every one,' and Mrs Swiller forced a kind of snorting laugh.

'No laughing matter,' said the Squire severely. 'Mrs Gobblespud?'

'Pigs can't swim, Squire, we all knows that,' said Mrs Gobblespud in a strained voice. 'Not if they'm normal,' she added thoughtlessly.

'Normal? Normal?' said the Squire loudly. 'What child of mine has ever been other than normal? What? Eh? What are you talking about? What's she talking about, Mrs Maizemunch?'

'Don't know, Squire.'

'Mrs Grazegrass?'

'Can't say, Squire.'

'Mrs Grubguzzle?'

'Don't ask me, Squire.'

'But I do ask you,' shouted the Squire angrily. 'I do ask you, dammit. I'm asking all of you. Except of course Mrs Barleylove,' and he shifted his gaze back to the door of Number Five.

Nobody said anything.

'Now lookee here,' said the Squire. 'If none of you ladies is willing or able to tell me about this business, I can only presume that it's connected with Mrs Barleylove, what?'

Still no one said anything.

'Well, she's at Resthaven, ain't she?' said the Squire. Eight heads nodded. The Squire began to lose patience again.

'You're not telling me,' he shouted, 'that Mrs Barleylove's been swimming in the brook, eh? What? What?'

Eight heads shook and eight faces struggled to keep straight at this question.

'Well then, dammit!' roared the Squire. 'I saw her last litter cross the yard with me own eyes, not a couple of days ago, and a damn fine bunch they were. Any father would be proud of them. And,' he added as an afterthought, 'any mother too. So if she's not swimming, and she's got no youngsters with her, will you kindly tell me who in the name of St Anthony is this swimming pig?'

Now St Anthony is the patron saint of pigmen, and when the sows heard the Squire swear so dreadfully, they knew that the issue could no longer be avoided. It would have had to have come out sometime. It had better come out now. Mrs Troughlicker, Mrs Boltapple, and Mrs Swedechopper looked inwards towards Mrs Swiller, Mrs Grubguzzle, Mrs Grazegrass, and Mrs Maizemunch looked inwards towards Mrs Gobblespud.

'Well?' said the Squire.

'Well, Squire,' said Mrs Swiller and Mrs Gobblespud together. 'This last litter, Mrs Barleylove . . . had a . . . dag,' they finished in a kind of whisper.

There was an awful silence, broken only by the sound of the Squire grinding his tusks. The sows could not see his eyes, hidden by his drooping ears, and of this they were glad.

At last he spoke, very softly. 'Go on,' he said.

Mrs Swiller swallowed. 'Usually, you see, Squire,' she said, 'when a . . . dag's born . . .'

'Usually?' interrupted the Squire in the same soft voice.

'Don't happen very often, of course,' put in Mrs Gobblespud hastily, 'but most of us, one time or another . . .'

'I see,' said the Squire heavily.

'And then,' said Mrs Swiller, 'the servant takes it away.'

'Takes it away?'

'Well, the mother never do see un no more.'

'But this un came back!' said Mrs Gobblespud excitedly, and at this the rest could not contain themselves but joined in in a babble of voices.

'I seen it!'

'Brave little love!'

'Wouldn't be beat!'

'Squeezed under the door!'

'Then Pigman come again!'

'Dirty fat man!'

'We told un!'

'And later on he come again!'

'When t'others crossed the yard!'

'And she told un!'

At last the hubbub died down, and there was silence again, this time unbroken.

After a while the Squire spoke. It seemed to the sows that he sounded old and tired.

'This . . . dag, then,' he said slowly, 'is down at

Resthaven with Mrs Barleylove, what?'

'Yes, Squire,' they all replied.

'It must be the swimmer, then?'

'Yes, Squire.'

'Extraordinary. Extraordinary. Boy or gel?'

'Boy, Squire.'

'Boy, eh? What's he called?'

'Daggie Dogfoot.'

'Daggie what?'

'Dogfoot.'

'Because . . .?'

'Yes, Squire.'

'Which is presumably how he . . .?'

Eight heads nodded, and nine brains imagined the scene in the brook. 'Extraordinary,' said the Squire. 'Extraordinary, what?'

His natural courtesy reasserted itself, and he said in his normal bluff hearty voice, 'I'm obliged to you, ladies. Pray return to your duties, doncherknow.'

But after the sows had disappeared from sight, the boar still leaned upon his gate. He felt shocked, as we all are when we learn home truths about ourselves. But he also felt in some way relieved, for it is better to admit some facts, even hard bitter facts, than to go on pretending that they don't exist. Most of all perhaps, as he stood there in the late afternoon sunshine, he began to feel proud.

Daggie Dogfoot, eh? he thought to himself. Taken

away but fought his way back, what? Wouldn't be beaten, doncherknow. And swimming! Swimming like a damned fish, apparently! Extraordinary! By St Anthony, said the Squire to himself, I'd like to meet the little chap.

CHAPTER 9

THE RACE

Daggie spent nearly all that day in the water, only coming out for a drink of milk or to eat some of the pig-nuts which the servant threw down. The pigman noticed nothing. We only see what we expect to see, and he did not dream that he was the slave of a swimming pig.

Mrs Barleylove had already come to look upon Felicity as a kind of combination of nurse, aunt, instructress and lifeguard. She stood upon the bank watching teacher and pupil with a silly grin on her big fat face.

Felicity concentrated on Daggie's streamlining, to begin with. She wanted him lower in the water, but he was having trouble with his nose. Like all pigs, his nostrils faced directly forwards out of the flat end of his snout and the water simply rushed up them.

'Why doesn't the water go up *your* nose?' spluttered Daggie, after much trial and error.

'Oh, we've got a sort of valve thing we can shut to stop it,' said the duck. 'Just like you can shut your eyes if you don't want to see something.' She paused, considering. 'Perhaps you've got one too?' she said.

'Try and see, my love,' called Mrs Barleylove. 'After all, my dear,' she addressed Felicity, 'I can put my snout deep in a trough full of slops, and gobble away without having to take it out.'

So Daggie tried, first on dry land, thinking very hard about pinching the insides of his nostrils together, while Felicity peered up his nose. After a bit she thought it was working so they went in the water, and it was!

Then Felicity redesigned Daggie's swimming action. His otter-like forefeet were just fine for the job; all he needed to be taught was to reach and pull instead of paddling. But his hindfeet, used as though running on dry land, hadn't the necessary drive.

The duck taught him a different method – to stick his hindlegs straight out behind him and beat them up and down in the water alternately, as fast as he could, keeping them stiff, barely breaking the surface.

They reached this stage by the end of the first day, and a long day it seemed to a very tired piglet curling up by his mother's warm side under the oak tree at dusk.

Oddly enough, as the Muscovy was settling to sleep on her alder branch, she heard, further up the valley, a thin hard cry in the coming darkness. 'I-zaak!' it sounded like, 'I-zaak!' Must warn Daggie about otters, she thought drowsily. Don't want him mistaken for a big fish.

For the next couple of days they worked hard at improving Daggie's style, and on the morning of the fourth day Felicity swam down early from her alder tree and found Daggie already practising in the pool. She hid behind some bulrushes and watched. Nor was she alone. From holes in the bank the blunt heads of water voles poked out. Moorhens peeped from among the reeds. The kingfisher sat on a brookside root, forgetting his fishing in his interest. And above, taking time off from mousing, a kestrel hung in fascination over the swimming pig.

He's good, thought Felicity, watching him slice through the water, low and straight, only his eyes and the dome of his head showing except when he tipped up his nostrils for a quick breath, hindlegs beating rhythmically, those curious forefeet pulling strongly. She left the bulrushes and swam into the pool.

'Hello, Felicity!' shouted Daggie. 'I've just been warming up. You said something about a final trial today.'

'Well,' said Felicity, 'I thought we might have a race. I mean you've taken to the water like a duck, as the saying goes. Let's see if you can beat one.'

'Hey, steady on!' Daggie said. 'You're a proper swimmer. You've been doing it all your life. I'm only a beginner. You'll wallop me.'

I'm not so sure of that, thought the Muscovy.

'It's only a bit of fun,' she said. 'Just to see how you perform over a longer distance. I thought we could start from the tail of the pool and swim upstream as far as the Resthaven boundary fence. The current's not running all that strongly because we haven't had rain for a long time. And it's a pretty straight course. About two hundred yards overall, I should think. OK?'

'I'm game!' said Daggie. 'Wait while I fetch Mammie to watch.'

'Well, don't bring her here,' said Felicity. 'Ask her if she'd be kind enough to go to the finish. Ask her to stand on the bank by the fence and act as judge.'

Five minutes later duck and pig floated side by side at the lower end of the pool, and, in the distance, they could see the big spotted shape of Mrs Barleylove come down to the bank and stand waiting. A little way up the kingfisher sat on his root.

'We'll use him as a starting signal,' said Felicity.
'When he moves, swim.'

They fixed their eyes on the blazing little bird, and
Daggie braced his hindfeet against the bank behind
him, ready to get a good push-off. He quivered all
over with excitement.

Suddenly, in a burning streak of colour, the
kingfisher flashed away upstream, and they were off!

For a time they were level, and Felicity, thrusting as
hard as she could with her broad webs, began to
think that she had overestimated this prodigy; for
though she could see from the corner of her eye that
he was swimming beautifully, doing everything that
he'd been taught in perfect style, she felt she had the

measure of him. For a moment she even considered slacking off a bit, to let him win and give him confidence. Then she caught his eye, and it seemed to have a twinkle in it.

Suddenly, at about the halfway stage, Daggie Dogfoot changed gear, and Felicity realized that he'd only been playing with her. Twice as low as before went his body in the water, twice as hard as before pulled those otter's feet, twice as fast as before beat those outstretched hindlegs, and he shot away in front of her with the speed of a salmon. She could hear Mrs Barleylove behaving as an impartial judge certainly should not, urging Daggie on to further efforts with loud proud squeals, and saw her jump for joy, all four feet off the ground, as he crossed the finishing line fifty yards ahead.

By the time the duck finished, the piglet had been able to climb out of the brook, shake himself all over, be licked by the judge, and call encouragement to his puffing panting teacher. He isn't even out of breath, thought Felicity as she clambered out and waddled up to mother and son.

'How about that then, missus?' she puffed. 'Aren't you proud of him?'

'Any mother would be,' said Mrs Barleylove. And any father too, she thought. At least I hope he will.

CHAPTER 10

IZAAK

A mile upstream was a mill, the very mill that ground the barley meal for the pigs, and beside it was a great pond that gave the water-power to drive the millwheel. It was from this pond, some nights before, that the thin hard cry had reached Felicity's ears as she dropped off to sleep. The animal that had made the cry was a big dog-otter, in the best of health and the worst of tempers. And the reason for his anger had been his lack of success in realizing a long-held ambition.

The mill-pond was deep and dark, with a bed made of thick mud and the rotting of a million leaves dropped into it over many autumns. Big fish lived in it, tench and carp and pike; and of these last there was one absolute monster, so otter-lore had it, a pike half as long as a man, as fierce as a wolf, and twice as cunning. Often in his travels between the sea and the hills, this particular otter had spent some time by the mill-pond with one idea in mind, to find this monster and kill him and eat him. And on that particular night he had come close to doing it.

Searching the deepest darkest corner of the thickest tangle of weeds, the otter had suddenly seen, motionless beneath him, a long barred shape with narrow wolf-jaws and cold hard eyes, a shape even longer than himself and he was thirty inches from the end of his nose to the tip of his rudder.

He twirled that rudder now and threw himself

over and down in a wonderful display of underwater aquabatics, and drove hard with all four webs. But, quick as he was, the long barred shape was quicker, leaving behind it a swirling fog of rotten leaves and a cloud of soupy water and strings of gas-bubbles and an angry otter.

'I-zaak!' the otter had cried in his fury as he hauled himself out by the black oak sluice-gates all slimy with mosses, 'I-zaak!'

The otter spent several days by the mill-pond, enjoying some easy fishing but without further sight of the monster pike, and then, on the day after Daggie and Felicity had had their race, decided to move on downstream. He felt like a trip to the sea, and some salty dabs and crabs to eat as a change from dull-fleshed pond-fish.

He slipped down with the last of the night, past the farm buildings, under Felicity asleep on her alder branch, past the finishing line of the race, and into the reach which led to the pool beneath the high bank. Sometimes he swam on the surface, sometimes only a string of bubbles showed his progress.

But suddenly he saw something which not only made him lift his round tom-cat's head right up out of the water, but actually land and stand up in the grass on his hindlegs, peering and sniffing and moving his head from side to side as though he simply could not believe his eyes. In the pool ahead, swimming rapidly from side to side with a racing turn at either bank, was a pig! It wasn't a very big pig by the look of it, no longer than the otter's body without its rudder, but it was, undoubtedly, a white pig with black spots. And it was, undoubtedly, swimming.

Now otters have a tremendous, if rather twisted, sense of humour, and they love jokes, especially bad jokes. One of the jokes that this otter enjoyed very much was giving people sudden awful frights. As everyone knows, a good way to give someone a sudden awful fright is to appear, from nowhere, when you're least expected, and better still, to make a fearful noise at the same time. A big grin came over the otter's face, and he dropped down and slid into and under the water.

Daggie was exactly in the middle of the pool, swimming along without a care in the world in the peaceful silence of the early morning, when suddenly, right beside him, a grinning whiskery face popped up, opened a wide mouth to show a battery of sharp white teeth, and shouted, right in his ear, 'I-ZAAK!'

Daggie felt three sorts of feelings, all at the same time. Startled, because of the sudden noise, afraid, because of the rows of teeth, and angry, because he was startled and afraid. Of the three he quickly decided that he was mostly angry, and he trod water and said in a shrill breathless voice, 'I don't know who you are but this is my pool and you've got no manners frightening people like that and I'll tell my Mammie and Felicity and they'll sort you out and anyway your breath stinks of fish.'

Now otters make all sorts of noises, from loud ones when they are angry or want to frighten someone, through chitterings and chatterings, to lovely flutey whistles when they are playing or calling to one another from afar. But when they think something is really very funny, they laugh quite silently.

To Daggie's astonishment, this is what the creature in front of him proceeded to do, splitting his hairy face wide open, and rocking to and fro in the water with his webbed forepaws clasped against his chest. He laughed so much and rocked about so wildly that eventually he sank below the water and swallowed some mouthfuls. Spitting and puffing, he came back to the surface, and, at last, calmed himself enough to speak to the piglet.

'Sorry, old pig,' he spluttered, still grinning broadly, 'sorry if I scared you.'

By now Daggie had got his breath back, and he said with a sort of quiet dignity, 'I'm not an old pig, I'm a young pig. And I'm not just a pig, I'm a pedigree Gloucester Old Spots. And my name is Daggie Dogfoot, son of Champion Imperial Challenger III of Ploughbarrow.'

The otter's mouth fell wider and wider open during this recital; but whether in astonishment or in preparation for another round of silent laughter Daggie never knew, for at that instant there was a whistle of wings and Felicity splashed down between them.

So busy had she been with Daggie's training that she had quite forgotten to mention the subject of otters to him, as she had realized with horror when this one's shout had woken her. Now she faced the danger bravely, determined to protect her little friend. There was a moment's pause, and then all three animals spoke at the same time.

'Are you all right, Daggie?' said Felicity. 'Who in the water is he?' said Daggie. And 'Hello, old duck,' said the otter, and dived beneath the surface.

As the friends swam rather rapidly to the Resthaven bank, they answered each other's questions.

'Yes, I'm all right,' said Daggie. 'Why shouldn't I be?'

'Because that's an otter,' said Felicity. 'Great hunter. Kills anything and everything that swims – fish, frogs, eels, ducklings. Never heard of it bothering piglets, but then piglets don't usually swim. Best keep well away from him.'

'Well, he didn't hurt me,' said Daggie. 'He just seemed to find me rather funny. I can't think why.'

As they talked, they could see strings of bubbles bobbing up as the otter searched the pool, and after a moment more he surfaced, smooth as oil, and walked out on to the sandy shallow below them.

'No fish in there, old pig,' said the otter cheerfully, 'and don't say there are 'cos there ain't. Must have driven them away with all that swimming practice of yours. What's a pig doing swimming anyway, old duck?'

'I taught him,' said Felicity shortly. 'What's your name, if I might ask?'

'Izaak,' said the otter. 'And don't think it ain't 'cos it is.'

Felicity's eyes began to twinkle. 'Izaak?' she said. 'After Izaak Walton?'

'Who's he, old duck?' said the otter.

'Oh, another famous fisherman,' said Felicity and she made her quot-quot-quotting noise.

'Never heard of him,' said the otter, 'and I know all the otters hereabouts and don't say I don't 'cos I do. No, mother called me that when I was a cub. On account of the noise I make when I'm a bit niggled. Or,' and he grinned, 'when I'm giving someone a sudden awful fright. Silly name. My friends call me Ike, and don't say they don't 'cos they do.'

There was something very nice about the otter, despite his fearful fishy breath. Perhaps it was his cheeriness. Perhaps it was his odd way of speaking. Or maybe it was the growing certainty that he was not in fact an enemy to them that made the two friends suddenly warm to him.

'Sorry I spoke so rudely to you, Mr Izaak,' said Daggie, 'but you did give me a sudden awful fright.'

'That's all right, old pig,' said the otter. 'I'm fond of a good laugh and don't say I ain't 'cos I am.' He turned to Felicity. 'Going back to this business of him' – he nodded at Daggie – 'swimming. From what I could see, he's pretty good on the surface. I never expected to see a pig swim, old duck, let alone swim as well as that, and don't say I did 'cos I didn't.'

'Yes, he is good,' said Felicity. 'But then he's lucky

enough to have been born specially equipped,' and she pointed with her bill at Daggie's forefeet.

'Let's have a look, old pig,' said the otter, and after a close examination he sat back with a long low whistle, and looked consideringly at the piglet.

'Tell you what,' he said. 'I was going to the seaside for a break, but I'm not in a hurry. Now am I right in thinking you haven't done much underwater work?'

'Not much,' said Daggie. 'Just the odd surface dive.'

'It's nearly all been surface work,' said Felicity. 'I'm afraid I'm not much good down below.'

'No, but I am,' said the otter.

'And don't say you aren't . . .' said Daggie quickly.

'. . . because you are,' finished Felicity, and they all laughed in their different ways, the otter silently, the duck quot-quotting, the piglet giving little squeals.

'Seriously,' said the otter, 'I could teach you a lot, old pig, if you'd like. You've got no webs, and no rudder worth speaking of, so you'll be a bit slow on the turn. But I could teach you a lot about breath control and use of currents and manoeuvrability and general aquabatics. We'd have you taking big fish in no time.'

'Well,' said Daggie doubtfully. 'I'd love to have lessons from you, Mr Izaak, but I don't actually eat fish.'

'Rubbish,' said Felicity sharply. 'You mean you

haven't eaten fish – yet. Just think, if this gentleman is kind enough to teach you . . . after all, pigs are omnivorous.'

'What's that mean, old duck?' said the otter.

'Means they can eat anything and everything.'

'She's clever, she is, ain't she, old pig?' said the otter. 'Mind you, they say eating fish is good for your brains, so you might get as clever as her. Though it doesn't seem to have done me much good,' and he rocked about in another fit of silent laughter.

So it came about that Daggie Dogfoot acquired a second teacher, and straightaway began another lot of lessons; so that by the time Mrs Barleylove, who had slept through everything, rolled down to the brook for her morning drink, she found that Daggie was more under the water than on it. And often when his head popped up there was a round brown whiskery one beside it and sometimes his squeaks of delight mingled with the stranger's lovely flutey whistles. Felicity explained everything to her, and, because it was all right with Felicity, it was all right with her.

Together they went to the top of the high bank and looked down. And in the clear waters of the pool they saw the wonderful submerged aquabatics of the otter as he rolled and curled and twisted and tied himself into a dozen different beautiful fluid knots; and close behind him, following and copying as best he could, was a fast-improving piglet.

78

All that day Daggie played with and learned from his new tutor, occasionally coming to the bank to see if his old tutor approved and was not upset; and she did and she wasn't; and his mother beamed her usual fatuous smile of pride.

In the afternoon swimmers and spectators moved upstream a little, and the otter caught a big trout, taking it in a lightning upward swirl too fast for the eye to follow. He pulled it out on to the bank and offered Daggie first bite ('From the shoulder; the flesh is sweetest there, old pig'). Daggie was too polite to refuse, and afterwards glad that he hadn't, for it was delicious. Between them they ate most of the best of it, as they were hungry from their exertions,

and, when they had returned to the brook, Mrs Barleylove ate the rest, head, tail, bones and all, till not a scale was left.

When the light began to fade, the otter said he must be going.

'See you tomorrow, old pig,' he said. 'You're learning fast.'

'Oh, I did enjoy that,' said Daggie. 'The underwater training, and the trout, and of course meeting you. Thank you so much, Mr Izaak.'

'Good-night, old pig,' said the otter. 'But I told you before, and don't say I didn't 'cos I did – my friends call me Ike.'

'Thanks, Ike,' said Daggie happily.

CHAPTER 11

THE FLOOD

Daggie did not in fact see his new friend Ike on the morrow, because overnight the weather, which controls everything in the countryside, changed completely. As Felicity had said before the race, they hadn't had rain for a long time. But not an hour after the otter had slipped away upstream, the heavens opened and proceeded to make up for their stinginess by such a display of generosity as none of the animals had ever known before. It rained very heavily all that night, and went on without stopping for two further days and nights.

The sows in their sties kept to their inner compartments, only venturing into their soaking outer runs for food. The Squire of course was dry under his verandah roof, but the constant stream of water flowing across the yard from higher ground worried him. He was not concerned for himself, but he couldn't help thinking about the strange son of whose existence he had only just heard. He hoped very much that that existence would not be ended in an untimely way, for he knew that boys will be boys, and this one sounded particularly adventurous. The brook will be very swollen, thought the Squire. I hope the little chap has the savvy to stay on dry land.

He spoke to the servant about it, but the pigman, more hideous than ever in yellow oilskins and sou'wester, was too stupid to understand his master.

At Number One and Number Two Mrs Troughlicker and Mrs Boltapple stood upright at their front doors and looked anxiously over the yard. It was covered with a stream of fast-running water, as indeed were the outer runs of all the sties. Only inside, where each sow had a raised wooden platform six inches high, was there still a dry space for them and their piglets. Mrs Troughlicker spoke first.

'I don't like it, Mrs B.,' she said in a worried voice. 'Never seed rain like this afore. Much more, and the young 'uns will be led in the wet.'

'Just what I was saying to Mrs Swedechopper next door,' replied Mrs Boltapple. 'Then they'll get chilled, and then . . .' She shuddered at her own thoughts.

'What can us do?' asked Mrs Troughlicker.

'I'll be butchered if I know,' swore Mrs Boltapple. 'If only the rain 'ud stop.'

But the rain did not stop. On the contrary, even as they spoke it began to come on heavily again, and the ladies hastily retreated indoors.

The pigman stood at the door of his meal-shed and looked down at the water, now almost over the lower of the two concrete steps. Behind him he heard rats squeaking among the bins and his red face grew redder at the sound of his enemies' voices. But even as he turned to reach up for his hardwood club and do battle, a big buck rat came running out of the gloom of the shed and scampered right over his Wellington boots and out of the door. It fell into the water and swam rapidly away down the yard. And as the pigman watched it open-mouthed, half a dozen more rats of all sizes dashed past him and into the water and away. Something he had heard long ago, at school perhaps, came into his mind. A sinking ship, he thought. Rats leaving a sinking ship.

At that instant the westerly wind, which had been blowing hard from the sea far down at the foot of the valley, dropped for a moment and in the ensuing lull the pigman heard a sound from the other direction, from the upper eastern end. It was a muttering that grew to a grumbling that grew to a mighty rumbling and, straining his eyes through the driving rain, he stared back up the line of the brook to where it curved into view round some trees two fields away.

Suddenly, to his horror, he saw a great wall of brown water coming around this bend and he knew in a flash what must have happened. The sluice-gates have gone, thought the pigman, the mill-pond's burst; and for once in his slow lumbering life he acted quickly.

Grabbing up a sack of pig-nuts, he jumped off the steps of the meal-house into the six-inch-deep water, and splashed his way to the sties. Door after door he flung open: Mrs Troughlicker's, Boltapple's, Swede-chopper's, Swiller's, missing the empty Number Five, then Mrs Gobblespud's, Maizemunch's, Graze-grass's, Grubguzzle's. As the sows and litters ran out into the yard, he blundered across it to the store pens and fattening pens, throwing wide door after door till a hundred and fifty spotted shapes of all sizes were stampeding about in the rushing flood. Only when he had opened the last door of all, the Squire's, did he allow himself one fearful glance over his shoulder. The wall of water was halfway across the last field before the buildings, and coming at the speed of a galloping horse.

The pigman, like all his kind, knew that pigs are the most awkward animals in the world to drive, so he did the only thing he could. Handicapped as he was by his bulk and his boots and his long yellow oilskins and the sack of pig-nuts, still he ran as hard as he could for the gate that led to Resthaven, shouting at the top of his voice the pig-keeper's universal feeding-call.

'Pig-pig-pig-pig-pig-pig-pig-pig-pig!' he yelled amidst the noise of the rain and the renewed wind and the thundering of the watery threat behind them; and he pounded desperately towards the high ground at the top of the little triangular field.

And behind him rose two waves. One was white, spotted with black, and one was brown. One squealed with fear, and one roared with menace. One was moving as fast as it possibly could, but a pig cannot gallop half as speedily as a horse, and the other wave gained and gained upon the first. As the

last and slowest piglet struck the rising ground, the first and fastest breaker of the flood was less than a sow's length from his curly little tail.

Then the flood turned before the steep, and swept across the lower slopes of the field, smashing down the old oak tree from the place where it had stood for three hundred years and carrying it away like a matchstick. Twenty feet above Daggie's take-off place on the high bank went the oak, twisting and turning and thrashing its old arms in agony on its road to the windswept sea.

But the pigs were safe, not just all one hundred and fifty-one of them, but all one hundred and fifty-three. For the first thing the pigman saw, when his pounding heart and bursting lungs had quieted a little, was a group of three figures standing at the very topmost point of Resthaven and staring at the great army of pigs covering the high slope. Old sow from Number Five's all right then, he thought. And that 'orrible little dag. Though the Lord knows what one of my ducks's doing with them.

There was noise all around them, as they stood and panted on their hilltop refuge. The blustering shout of the wind competed with the menacing roar of the brook that had become a great river. On the waters of that river hissed the lash of the never-ending rain. At one moment Daggie fancied he heard, far out on the flood, an excited flutey whistle, as though someone was actually enjoying the storm. But suddenly, clear above the other noises, was heard a sharp cracking sound, and from the hill a hundred and fifty-five heads turned and three hundred and ten eyes looked back towards the homes they had left behind, to see the beginning of the first voyage of a strange craft.

The rats had been right to go, for the cracking noise proclaimed the launching of the pigman's meal-shed, as the floods lifted it bodily from its foundations. Past the drowned sties it came, over the submerged field-gate, and out into the centre of the great expanse of dark sliding eddying water that now stretched before the watchers. Its door hung open, as the pigman had left it when he ran to rescue them, and as the shed spun slowly in the current they could see within it the great bins of barley meal and middlings and flaked maize and the piled sacks of pig-nuts, all sailing swiftly away to be food for the fish in the sea.

Another story came into the pigman's slow mind from distant days in the village schoolroom. Looks like the Ark, he thought. Trouble is, we ain't on it. And all the food I got for 'em is this here half hundredweight of nuts. Still, they won't be short of a drink.

He went to the topmost point of Resthaven, and, opening the sack, threw the pig-nuts far and wide over the small triangle of field that was left high and dry. Within half a minute everything was eaten, and the multitude was squealing for more, while far in the distance the meal-shed sailed on downriver.

The pigman folded the empty sack, placed it on top of an ant heap, and sat carefully down upon it. He sat motionless, his head in his hands, while the pigs jostled and grumbled below him. Had there been anyone on any of the other hilltops nearby, it would have seemed a strange sight: above, the bright yellow spot of the man's oilskins and sou'wester; below that, the spotted throng; and below them, the chocolate-coloured flood, darkening from milk to plain as the daylight faded. Mrs Barleylove and Daggie and Felicity still stood together.

'Poor old Duckman,' said Felicity, 'he looks all in.'

'Duckman?' said Daggie absently. 'Oh, you mean Pigman. Yes, he does. Still, he's a good and faithful servant, you know. He did his duty.' Felicity had also been thinking of the story of the Flood, as the ark-like meal-shed had drifted by, but, being better educated than the man, remembered more of it. She began to make the quot-quot-quotting noise which Daggie now knew well was her way of giggling.

'What's the joke?' said Daggie.

'I was thinking of a story,' said Felicity. 'In a book. Called the Bible. About a man called Noah.'

'Why?' said Daggie. 'Is Pigman like Noah?'

'No,' said Felicity. 'More like one of his sons.'

'What was he called?' asked Daggie.

'Ham,' said Felicity happily.

CHAPTER 12

GOING FOR HELP

In the early light of the following morning the scene was quite different, To begin with, the flood was not quite as high, for the burst pond was empty now and it had not rained in the night. The water had receded far enough to show the gaping hole where the old oak used to stand, but it was still running very wide and very strong, and there was no sign of the outline of the brook.

The other difference was one of colour. The hill-tops around showed brilliantly green in the light of the early morning sun, but what there was to see of Resthaven was blacky-brown, and moving and milling upon it were blacky-brown creatures.

Pedigree Gloucester Old Spots they might be, but no one would have known, for the herd had rooted and routed over every square inch, looking for something, anything, to eat, and they were plastered in dirt.

As the pigman had said, there was no problem about drinking, for millions and millions of gallons of water flowed by them. It was food they were thinking about, and the first thing they had done was to graze off every blade of grass and gobble up every dock and nettle, every thistle even; every leaf and shoot which they could reach through the boundary pig-wire they had torn off and, where a hedgerow tree was close enough, had chewed its bark. Then they had turned up the whole top triangle of the field and ferreted out the roots of every blade of grass, every patch of clover, every weed. Anything they came across went down them – worms, slugs, beetles, even some families of fieldmice, babies and all; and of all the hundreds of ant heaps which had dotted the upper slopes of Resthaven only one remained, and on it, yellow against the blacky-brown background, the pigman still sat, head hanging, shoulders bowed, stomach rumbling with hunger.

Mrs Barleylove and Daggie were just as black and filthy as the rest, for they too had been rootling everywhere for food. Only Felicity was spotlessly clean, not a black nor a white feather out of place, for she of course had flown out on to the flood for a

thorough wash and brush-up. She stood now on Mrs
Barleylove's broad back, to be out of the way of the
pushing, shoving, squealing multitude of earth-
covered pigs, and spoke into the big droopy ear, softly
so as not to be overheard.

'Look, missus,' she said. 'We've got to do
something, you know as well as I do. This lot's so
hungry they're eating anything now. It only needs a
little piglet to get trodden on and they'll gobble him
up. And then they'll start on one another. I'm right,
aren't I?'

Mrs Barleylove shuddered. She knew how every
pig worships food, and she was well aware, though

she didn't know the word, that pigs are omnivorous, eating everything that is remotely edible. She remembered stories that her mother had told her of swill-feeding in the old days, when rats, and sometimes cats, would fall into the swill tubs and get cooked; the pigs would champ them up quite happily, her mother said.

"Course you'm right, my dear,' she said quietly. 'We got to get help. We got to get food. But how? It don't look like the servant can swim or he'd have bin gone. And tidn't much good you going, if you'll excuse me; people wouldn't connect a Muscovy duck with a herd of pigs. The only one that can swim, after all, is . . .' and she stopped, and her mouth fell open.

'Oh no!' cried Mrs Barleylove. 'Oh no! Not him!'

'It's got to be your Daggie,' said Felicity. 'If nobody goes, and no one comes to find you all, and the floods don't go down, for a week say, there's going to be all Hell let loose here.'

'But he may be drowned!' wailed Mrs Barleylove.

'I don't think so,' said Felicity, 'though I grant that it's a possibility. As against the probability,' she said very slowly and clearly, 'that if he stays here, he'll be . . . eaten.'

There was a small silence between them, in the middle of the uproar of empty-bellied pigs.

'All right,' grunted Mrs Barleylove at last. 'If he's

willin', bless his little heart,' and she blinked her white-lashed eyes very quickly. 'But you'll go with him, my dear, won't you? Please?'

'Of course,' said Felicity. 'Try not to worry, missus. I'm sure it'll all have a happy ending. If we can find some other servants like Duckman, er, Pigman, I mean, somewhere downstream, they'll see Daggie's spots and they'll know where he's from. After all, there's only this one herd of Gloucester Old Spots in the district, isn't there?'

'Far as I know,' said Mrs Barleylove.

'Well then,' said the duck, 'they'll know something's wrong. And they'll get food up somehow, by boat, or helicopter.'

The sow had no notion what a helicopter was, but she had a lot of faith in Felicity, and she called loudly for her son.

Daggie came running up, black as the ace of spades. He was very hungry, for his mother's milk had dried up now, and he had been pushed and shoved away from anything that looked like food by his stronger brethren. But his eyes were bright and his courage was high, and as soon as the plan was told to him, he was wild to go.

Felicity flew down to the water's edge, and Mrs Barleylove followed, barging her way through the press of pigs with Daggie at her heels. 'Make way! Make way!' she shouted, and the other sows, hearing her voice, pushed forward to see what was happening.

They were all asking questions at once when sharp squeals from above made them look round, and they saw the Squire come rolling down towards them, his tusks showing white in his muddy face as he tossed the stores and fatteners out of his way.

'What's going on?' he asked in his deep voice when he reached the sows. 'Mrs Barleylove, dear lady, what's going on, what?'

''Tis my son, Squire,' replied Mrs Barleylove proudly. 'He's going for help. He's going to swim for help, to find someone to bring us food.'

Those nearest to her heard her words, and as the news spread the herd fell silent, and every head was turned to listen.

'Your son?' said the Squire loudly. 'Your son?'

'Our son, Squire,' said Mrs Barleylove softly, feeling her white parts turn pink, and thankful for the mud that hid them.

'That's better,' said the Squire, and turning to the little piglet he looked curiously at him. Little shrimp, he thought, he's not much bigger than a rat. And those front feet . . .

He spoke quietly now, so that the pigs at the edge of the press raised their heads to hear the better, as the great boar looked down upon the little dag.

'So you're Daggie Dogfoot, what?' said the Squire.

'Yes, sir,' said Daggie politely.

'And you're going for help, are ye, boy?'

'Yes, sir.'

'Current's strong, ye know. Water's deep. Understand you can, er, swim pretty well, but it'll be damned dangerous, doncherknow. What?'

'Oh, I'll be all right,' said Daggie. 'Thank you, Father,' he added daringly. The boar cleared his throat as though there were some kind of lump in it.

'Well, good luck, my son,' he said in a loud strained voice. 'By St Anthony, I wish you the very best of good luck.'

And all around the mob of pigs echoed him. 'Good luck! Good luck!' they cried, and the pigman got up off his ant heap at the noise, and lumbered down to find out what it was all about.

He was just in time to see Daggie walk out into the shallows, the mud dissolving as the edge of the current began to wash him clean. Soon he was swimming, once again a white piglet with black spots, and then he was in midstream and the full force of the floodwater took him and whirled him away.

But every pig could see how beautifully he swam, and most of them could hear his farewell cry, and one of them stood alone, belly-deep in the shallows while a great tear ran down each of her fat cheeks and plopped into the stream. Come back safely, my Daggie, said Mrs Barleylove to herself.

Just then Felicity came flying back, low over the heads of the herd. The pigman had taken off his hat, the better to scratch his head in his utter bewilderment at the sight of a swimming pig, and Felicity dived down, caught it in her clawed feet and tore it from him.

'I'll take this with me,' she shouted to Mrs Barleylove, as she wheeled to follow Daggie. 'Maybe someone will know who this belongs to,' and she flew rapidly away, the sou'wester dangling below her, while the pigman danced in anger.

'Dratyer!' he cried, and 'Dangyer!' and 'Blastyer!',

shaking his huge fist at the two fast disappearing figures.

'Stupid iggerant duck!' he shouted. 'You and that 'orrible little dag, you make a fine pair. Never be no use to no one, not neither of you, nohow!'

And as the pigs ran to the topmost part of Resthaven, they caught a final glimpse of Daggie Dogfoot, far down on the flood. They could see Felicity for a little longer as she flew low, directly above the swimmer. And then there was nothing to be seen but a great waste of waters.

CHAPTER 13

Man on a Raft

Jumping about in anger had woken the pigman's brain from the daze of hopelessness into which it had fallen, and he began to think what he could do about the situation. It occurred to him, as it had to the duck much earlier, that there would be trouble with a capital T if the pigs remained unfed. His meal-shed, he knew, was gone, and help, if it ever came, might be a long time arriving; but after much headscratching, a simple idea came to him. Resthaven after all was only one side of the little conical hill on which they were marooned, so that there must be grass, and bushes, and trees round the back of this island in the floods. All he had to do was to take down the pig-netting that confined his herd, and then they could at any rate find something to keep them going.

To do this was not at all easy, since the fence had been well made in the first place, tightly stretched, and nailed to stout posts or sapling trees. Wire-cutters would have done the job in a minute but of course he had none with him. As he stood and looked at the fence, the Squire rolled up and stood beside him. They conversed in their separate languages.

'If only you had the brains, old fellow,' said the pigman, 'you'd get your great head under the wire and lift it up.'

'If you had any sense at all, Pigman,' said the Squire, 'you'd use that branch that's lying there as a lever to get the bottom of this wire up far enough for me to put my head under it.'

'If I had something for a lever,' said the pigman, 'I might be able to lift the bottom of it a bit. Then perhaps this daft old boar might see what I'm at.'

'Man's a fool,' said the Squire.

'Oh, there's a branch,' said the pigman. 'That might do.'

'Feller's tumbled to it at last,' said the Squire with a sigh, as the pigman slid the branch under the lowest-but-one strand of the pig-wire, stuck the far end into the ground beyond, and began to heave upwards. With great effort he managed to lift the bottom strand six inches above the gro und.

'Ladies!' shouted the Squire. 'I want you all on parade, please. Chop-chop!' and when the nine sows came galloping up, he said more quietly, 'spread out please. Four to one side of me, five to the other. Snouts down. Wait for my word.' And from the corner of his mouth he snarled at the servant, 'Come on, man. Put your back into it, what?'

Almost as though he could understand, the pigman redoubled his efforts; the bottom of the wire rose a fraction higher, the boar got his head under the lowest strand, then the sow on either side of him, and so on, until all ten heads were under and all ten great bodies tensed.

'Ready! Steady! Heave!' shouted the Squire, and with a twanging tearing noise a twenty-foot stretch of pig-wire rose up, up, up, till the retaining fence-posts popped out of the ground.

'Forward!' bawled the Squire, and before the advancing weight of more than four thousand pounds of pig the fence burst like a rotten tennis-net, and the rest of the herd poured through. Off round the back of the hill they went, snatching at the fresh grass like mad things, and the pigman was left alone.

The sight of his animals eating again reminded him painfully how empty his own stomach was. If only I had a boat, he thought, and he strained his little piggy eyes upstream as though wishing would make one appear. He did not see one, of course, but he did see something, two things in fact. They were about ten feet apart, halfway between him and his drowned buildings, and he suddenly realized that they were the tops of the gate-posts at the entrance to Resthaven.

Gate-posts, he thought. Water must have gone down a little bit, couldn't see them before. Gate-posts, he thought. There's a gate between 'em. Gate, he thought. Made of wood. Wood, he thought. Floats. Floats, he thought. Like a boat, well, like a raft.

He went down to the water's edge, and began to wade back towards the gate-posts. The current was strong but the pigman was powerful, and he fought his way along, deeper and deeper as he went down the slope. He was shoulder deep when at last he stood between the posts and, feeling underwater, found nothing. For a moment he felt only disappointment and anger, thinking that the flood had carried the gate away. Then he realized that of course it had been open when the waters had first burst upon it, hard on the heels of the fleeing herd; so that now it would be pointing downstream, as a flag streams out before the wind. He felt to one side and found it.

Now was the moment of decision for the pigman.

As Mrs Barleylove had guessed, he could not swim. Moreover, he was frightened of the very water. As a child, he had once been taken to the seaside on a school outing, but nothing would persuade him to go beyond the ripples. What he was doing now was, for him, an act of great bravery. But more was needed. In order to grip the heavy gate and clear it from the hanging-post, he would need, at this depth, actually to put his head under the dreaded water!

And if he lifted it free, would it bear him? And if it bore him, where to? To food, and shelter, and help?

Or out to the endless sea? Desperate men do desperate things, and the pigman closed his eyes, settled his feet firmly, and took a good grip and a deep deep breath.

There followed a scene which would have seemed pure comedy, had there been a human watcher unaware of the underlying drama; but for the pigman it could so easily have been one of tragedy.

To begin with, the hinges were jammed upon the hanging-pins, and it took three increasingly breathless dips below the surface before his utmost efforts could lift the gate free. And when it was free, the current immediately dragged it away, so that the pigman had to make a wild, belly-flopping leap at it as it went. He caught the back end of it, whereupon it tipped up like a live thing, threatening to throw him off into deeper water. Somehow, gasping, spluttering, panic-stricken, he managed to scramble further on to it, expecting all the time that it would submerge beneath him.

But it bore him, just, though the weight of the heavy man and his waterlogged clothes pushed it below the surface; so that he would have appeared, had there been a watcher, to be floating motionless upon the flood, like a bright yellow hippopotamus.

This was what he looked like to the first eyes that did see him. Most of the herd were on the reverse side of the hill, rooting and tearing anything they could find, but the Squire and Mrs Barleylove had not moved far from the break in the fence, and it was they who witnessed the pigman's progress.

'By St Anthony!' the Squire burst out. 'It's the damned servant! Seems to be lyin' on top of the water. Extraordinary! Feller can't be as stupid as I thought.'

Mrs Barleylove watched as the current bore the pigman steadily away. Daggie, she thought, where are you, my love?

'Going to have a look myself,' said the Squire, reading her thoughts. 'When the level drops a bit more. So I can see the line of the hedges or fences. Should be easy to bust 'em.'

'Easier with two, Squire,' said Mrs Barleylove.

Champion Imperial Challenger III of Plough-barrow raised his heavy head and gazed at this wife of his with approval and affection. 'Couldn't wish for a better partner,' he said. 'And try not to worry too much about the lad. We'll find him. You'll see.'

CHAPTER 14

ON THE DAM

Not long after Daggie and Felicity had disappeared from the sight of the watching herd, the course of the flood took a turn in a new direction and the course of their fortunes a turn for the better. A mile or so from Resthaven the old brook had rounded the foot of a high spur, plunged, south-west and seawards, into quite a deep steep valley and, though now swollen to many times its usual width, was nonetheless narrower at this point than the broad waters on which Daggie had begun his swim. Consequently the speed of the current increased dramatically, so that Felicity needed to fly at her fastest to keep up with the swimmer.

Daggie of course was too excited to be frightened. 'Weeeeeee!' he yelled as the racing water swept him along, but the Muscovy, ten feet above him, suddenly saw trouble ahead.

Something was blocking the way, a kind of rough dam, it seemed, though she could not yet see what it was made of; but she could see that the rushing flood parted before it, swirled away to either side, and fell from sight in a boiling swirl. Felicity knew something about waterfalls and the terrible down-currents beneath them, and she instantly realized the awful danger for Daggie should he be swept over.

Flying her hardest, she dropped low over the piglet, the strings of the yellow sou'wester held tight in her claws, the bonnet hanging low.

'Grab it in your teeth, Daggie!' she shouted. 'Quick! Don't argue!', and as soon as she felt his weight she turned and faced upstream, beating her wings with all her strength.

Try as she might she could still feel herself being dragged backwards but at least she was cutting down Daggie's breakneck speed and keeping him dead centre, on line for the obstruction; and when a hasty glance over her shoulder told her the moment was ripe, she turned and dropped down on to a branch that stuck out at water level. Pulling as hard as she could while walking backwards along this, she landed Daggie as an angler lands a fish. They were safe on

the dam, and behind and below them they could
hear the thunder of falling water.

Its purpose served, the yellow sou'wester slipped
over the falls on the start of a journey that was to
bring help, for someone spotted it far downstream
and fished it out, and inside it they could still just read
the pigman's name and address in his horrible scrawl.

'Gosh, that thing tasted nasty,' panted Daggie,
wrinkling his snout. 'What was that all about,
Felicity?'

Felicity looked at him and made her quot-quot-
quotting noise.

'Oh, nothing,' she said. 'I just thought we'd have a
breather. Let's take a look round.'

Curiously, perhaps because he was so breathless, sight was the last of Daggie's five senses to send messages to his brain. With the roar of the falls in his ears and the sour taste of oilskin in his mouth, the next thing he realized, through his sensitive forefeet, was that the bark of the big branch on which he was standing was familiarly rough, as though he had met, not just that kind of tree, but this particular tree before. Then suddenly, lifting his snout to the wind, he smelt food! And not just food, but pig-food! And not just pig-food somewhere miles away, but pig-food near, very near, here, right on this jumble of objects in the middle of the stream! Then at last – and all this happened in a matter of seconds – he used his eyes. What he suddenly saw excited him so much that he nearly lost his perch and fell off into the water again.

'Look, Felicity!' he shouted. 'Look – behind you!'

And there, jammed among the branches, was the meal-shed. It was still upright, its door still hung open, and out of the door came the wonderful smells. Like shipwrecked mariners stumbling upon treasure, they scrambled madly towards it.

Inside, the great bins of barley meal and middlings and flaked maize still stood, their wooden lids tight shut and far too heavy to be lifted by piglet or duck. But that did not matter, for on the floor was a great stack of sacks of pig-nuts and about the edge of the stack were bags that had fallen as the meal-shed had tossed on the flood. Some of these had broken open so that a part of the floor was covered in a rich dark-brown carpet of nuts which Daggie rushed upon and some of this carpet had been wetted into a beautiful mush by water seeping through the floorboards, so that Felicity could suck up a kind of lovely pig-nut porridge. For a long time there was nothing to be heard in the meal-shed but the sounds of eating.

Felicity stopped eating first, because her crop was full; she went out to the edge of the dam for a drink and, when her thirst was satisfied, flew round to take a look at the far side of the obstruction. She found, as she had suspected, that the jam of timber had caused a wicked waterfall down which Daggie would surely have plunged to a horrid death.

When she came back into the meal-shed, he was still eating. At last he staggered out and picked his way to the water and drank deeply. Returning, he let out a huge belch followed by a long sigh of contentment, flopped upon his side on the floor, and fell fast asleep, his little spotted balloon of a tummy rising and falling. Not a bad idea, thought the Muscovy, closing her eyes.

An hour or so later Daggie woke suddenly with a shout of 'Mammie!' A series of muddled dreams had turned into a nightmare, something to do with his babyhood; and sure enough, the very first thing he focused upon was the hardwood club, still hanging on its rusty nail. Then he saw the kind face of his friend Felicity looking down at him from the top of a meal bin, and remembered what had happened. Looking out of the door, he saw a big branch which stuck up in the air; and on the branch were familiar crinkly-edged leaves; and among the leaves were some acorns.

'It's the oak, isn't it, Felicity?' he said. 'It's the old oak from Resthaven.'

'Yes,' said the duck. 'It jammed across this narrow place, against some rocks probably, and then caught

everything else that came down, including, thank goodness, this shed.'

'Gosh, yes,' said Daggie. 'What a bit of luck. What super grub. I feel a new piglet.'

'You look a new piglet,' said Felicity. 'Your mother wouldn't recognize you.'

Daggie's mood changed instantly. 'Mammie!' he cried, jumping to his feet. 'Oh, Mammie! Oh, how selfish I am! Here I am, making a pig of myself, and all the time Mammie's hungry, starving perhaps. And Father. And my aunties. And my brothers and sisters. And all the others. Oh, what a selfish pig I am!'

'Don't be silly,' said Felicity shortly. 'It's only sensible that as we've been lucky enough to find all this food, we should eat our fill. We must keep up our strength, you know. There's an awful lot to do.'

'Yes, I suppose so,' said Daggie, a little less miserably. 'But what can we do? How can we get this food back to the others? We can't carry it.'

'I don't know,' said Felicity. 'I honestly don't know. But I've got a feeling that something will turn up.' And she began to preen herself and to rearrange her feathers, while Daggie lay down again on his distended stomach and gazed out of the door.

And as he gazed, something did turn up. At first Daggie could not see clearly what it was, for the sun was in his eyes: all he noticed was a yellowish lump in the distance, coming down towards them; a dead tree perhaps, he thought. But as it came nearer he could see that it was not vegetable but animal, that it was not dead but alive, for it had a staring white face and wide flaring nostrils and its teeth were bared in a grin of fear, while its tongue licked nervously over its thick lips; its body, he could now see, was bright yellow, and it seemed to ride effortlessly upon the surface.

'Felicity!' yelled Daggie in an agony of terror. 'A monster! A monster! He's coming straight for us!'

Felicity waddled to the door.

'I hope he is,' she said. 'We need him. It's Duckman.'

CHAPTER 15

Breakfast and Bed

The pigman, low in the water, did not realize the danger ahead. Even if he had, it is doubtful that he could have done much about it, so paralysed was he with terror. All he was concerned with was hanging on to his gate like grim death. This in fact was the saving of him, for when the current took hold and whirled him off to one side of the dam and over the falls, he held tight; had he let go then, he would probably have been sucked under by the downcurrents in the pool below and drowned.

Felicity, flying round to the other side of the dam, saw the man and his raft plunge down beneath the boiling surface; but then the heavy wooden gate rose again, its rider still clinging to it, water cascading off the soaking yellow oilskins. Once he's clear of the pool down there and out in midstream again, he'll be gone, with nothing to stop him between here and the sea, thought Felicity. But at that moment a freakish current dragged the gate back towards the dam, towards a point indeed where a strong branch of the old oak stuck out invitingly.

'If only he'd let go of the gate and grab that branch,' shouted the Muscovy over the noise of the falls to Daggie, who was standing above watching, 'otherwise he'll be gone in a minute.'

Inspiration came to Daggie.

'Scratch his hands, Felicity,' he yelled. 'Fly down and scratch his hands. That'll make him let go!'

As the piglet looked on, she flew down, pitched on the end of the gate, and deliberately dragged her sharp claws across the backs of the pigman's tightly gripping hands. Then everything happened at once. The pigman loosed his hold with a yell of pain and anger, and grabbed frantically at the branch. The gate shot from under him, caught the force of the stream again, and sailed steadily away. The duck flew back up on to the dam and perched beside Daggie.

Side by side, the friends watched anxiously as the pigman struggled to pull himself along the branch to safety. His clothes were soaked, his boots full of water, his tired limbs cramped, his hungry body chilled. But he was strong and he was desperate, and at last, somehow, he scrambled on to the dam.

For a while he lay in the tangle of timber, gasping for breath. When at last he sat up and looked about him, he saw the two watchers, and some colour came back into his wet white face.

'Dratyer!' he cried, shaking his bleeding fists at them, and 'Dangyer!' and 'Blastyer!'

Then, suddenly, he lurched to his feet. His mouth, open from the last shout, gaped wider still, his piggy eyes glinted, and in a kind of mad blundering stumble he began to clamber over the mess of timber in the direction of the two animals.

Hurriedly the stupid iggerant duck and the 'orrible little dag moved out of the way, but they soon realized the reason for the servant's excitement. Pigman had seen the back of the meal-shed.

Above everything else, the pigman was hungry, excruciatingly, ravenously hungry. For most of the thirty-odd hours which had passed since he ran from this shed in the face of the approaching flood, he had thought of food in general, and in particular of a packet of sandwiches left in the pocket of his old coat (the very pocket which had once carried Daggie) which hung from a second rusty nail beside the hardwood club. Ham sandwiches they were, his favourites, and the spittle ran down over his three chins as he fought his way round to the door.

He clambered in, and there was the coat. He plunged his great hand in the pocket, and there were the sandwiches. He tore off the paper in which they were wrapped and crammed them into his mouth. By the time Daggie and Felicity had summoned up courage to peep round the door, the sandwiches were gone, for there were only two of them, meant for a mid-morning snack. As they watched, the pigman broke open a sack of pig-nuts, picked out a handful, and began to chew them. A considering look came over his face, then something like a smile, and then he sat down and began to stuff himself.

'Gosh, he must be full,' said Daggie after a while. 'What d'you think he'll do next?'

'Don't know what to think,' said Felicity. 'First he comes floating down the river like a duck . . .'

'. . . and then he makes a pig of himself!' laughed Daggie. 'Extraordinary feller, doncherknow!' he said in a passable falsetto imitation of his father, and they both giggled in a chorus of little grunts and quot-quot-quotting noises.

The pigman had in fact decided what to do next. He had never had a deep thought in his whole life, but when certain simple ideas occurred to him he acted upon them without further ado.

Just at the moment his stomach was full, but the rest of his body was wet and cold and tired. His brain therefore received three messages. Get dry. Get warm. Get sleep.

The two heads looking round the door again saw the pigman move slowly into action. First he took off his yellow oilskins and hung them on a third rusty nail beside the old coat and the hardwood club. Then he opened the three great wooden meal-bins one after the other, and looked into each long and earnestly, scratching his head like mad. At the last, the flaked maize bin, he took off his gum-boots, emptied the water out of them on to the floor, and then solemnly filled them full of the crackly golden stuff.

Next he went to the middlings bin. He took off his trousers, his pullover, his shirt, and his socks, and carefully buried them all deep in the brown sawdusty stuff.

Lastly the pigman went to the barley meal bin, a strange sight now clothed only in enormous thick woolly greyish combinations. Laboriously, with much grunting, he climbed into the bin and began to work himself down into the thick white powdery stuff like some giant lugworm burying itself in soft sand. When he was waist deep in it, he reached up to a shelf above for a bundle of old copies of *The Pig Breeder's Gazette*. He wriggled on down till he was shoulder deep. Then he slipped the magazines under his head, plunged his arms under the barley blanket, and lay back with a sigh.

'By St Anthony,' said Daggie mischievously as the pigman closed his eyes, 'feller's actually goin' to sleep, what, what?' and they both burst out into another fit of the giggles.

CHAPTER 16

DREAMS

'Water's actually goin' down a bit, what, what?' said the Squire at precisely the same moment. 'Take a look at those young porkers over there, Mrs Barleylove. They're grazin' grass that was under water a couple of hours ago.'

By now the hungry herd had eaten everything growing on the little hill of which Resthaven formed a part so that the whole of it was now a blacky-brown hump; but at its edges a fresh green rim kept appearing as the flood level gradually dropped and as fast as it appeared the herd ate it off. The vegetable matter kept them going, but such a diet was rather like humans living on nothing but soggy lettuce, and they longed for solid substantial food.

'Couldn't us try to get downstream now, Squire?' said Mrs Barleylove. Her belly ached for a square meal and her heart ached for Daggie. The Squire heard the note of pleading in her voice, and nodded his heavy head.

'Not long now, dear lady,' he said. 'Don't fancy either of us as swimmers, doncherknow, so we must be able to keep in our depth. But you can see the line of the willows that mark the brook's edge pretty clearly now. And the tops of some fences.'

He thought for a moment. Then he gave his deep coughing grunt, and shouted 'Ladies! This way, please. Chop-chop!', and when the other eight sows had joined Mrs Barleylove, and all were standing round him in a respectful circle, he addressed them thus.

'Listen carefully please, ladies. Don't want to have to repeat myself. Now, it doesn't look as though help is coming. On the other trotter, water's dropping. Not enough yet to get the youngsters downstream, but Mrs Barleylove and I are going to take a little stroll and see what we can find.' He paused. 'Any objections?' he barked, but the sows noticed the fierceness of his look and said nothing.

'Right then,' said the Squire. 'Look after the herd. And ladies, one last thing. Do not attempt to follow us,' and he waded off, breast-deep, Mrs Barleylove in his wake.

Back at the meal-shed, everyone was now asleep and dreaming. Felicity dreamed her usual simple happy kind of dream, all peace and warm sunlight and dancing water.

The pigman's dream was more complex, and, like his waking thoughts, concerned food. In it he was collecting together all the things in the shed which he needed – matches, paper sacks and boxes to start a fire, a big square tin for a container, the bottle of vegetable oil which he used to shine his show pigs. A dream-smell of roast sucking-pig ran up his flaring nostrils, and he stirred restlessly in the barley meal bin, his white-lashed eyelids fluttering.

Daggie was having a nightmare. He lay in a pool of sunlight by the door, but in his mind he was back in Resthaven, before the flood, playing King of the Castle, jumping on Mammie's big stomach. Outside the meal-shed, the real sun disappeared behind a cloud bank, and the pool of sunlight was no more. And in his dream, too, the day turned grey, and his Mammie vanished, and something horrible was coming towards him, something huge, and fat, and white.

The pigman had settled so low in the barley meal that eventually he snored some of the floury stuff right up his nose. He woke up and rubbed at his face

with his mealy hands, so that he was white from top
to toe. His brain received a message. I am thirsty. He
levered himself out of the bin.

Then everything happened at once. Daggie woke
and squealed with terror as his nightmare became
reality. Felicity woke, and thinking her friend to be in
danger, flew at the pigman's head. The pigman put
up his hands to ward her off, tripped as the piglet
dashed between his legs, stubbed his toes in the
doorway, caught his foot in a branch outside and, like
a great tree falling, crashed into the water and sank
below the surface.

As Daggie and Felicity watched, horrified, they

saw on the far bank two great spotted figures galloping down towards the pool, and they heard in the distance a strange clattering noise.

The pigman's head broke water. 'Heeeelp!' he roared. 'Heee-gurgle-glug!' and down he went again.

CHAPTER 17

THE GREAT
STRANGE BIRD

Back at Resthaven, things were looking up. To be more exact, pigs were looking up, at a great strange bird in the sky.

They had heard the bird before they had seen it, for it had a loud rattling voice, and they raised their heads and watched it appear over the eastern hills. It flew down the valley towards them, pausing over the mill with its ruined pond, and again over the farm buildings, now almost empty of water. Its glassy eyes twinkled in the bright sunlight and its wings whirled above its body at great speed.

Suddenly it saw the herd in Resthaven, and it darted sideways towards the pigs and hovered above the little hill like some huge hawk, so low that they could feel the terrible wind of it. None of the pigs had ever seen a helicopter before and they galloped about in panic. But the bird came no lower, so they gathered in a nervous huddle and watched as a hole appeared in its side and a brown object fell out of it.

'It's layin' eggs on us!' shouted Mrs Grubguzzle in alarm, but before the words were out of her mouth the brown object hit the ground and burst open. A familiar smell came wafting to the snouts of the herd, growing stronger by the minute as two, four, eight more sacks of pig-nuts were tipped from the door of the helicopter. Then it turned and slid away westwards down the line of the brook.

When the helicopter reached the dam, the strangest scene met its glassy eyes. If it had really been a bird, it would have had the tallest of tall stories to tell to its children. As it was of course, there were three men in it, the pilot, the observer, and the winchman. And in later years, when they had children of their own, old enough for story-telling, they all told the same tale to their goggle-eyed families.

It was during the Great Summer Flood, they said, when people and animals in that part of the country had been cut off from supplies. Alerted by the discovery of the yellow sou'wester, they had been sent to an isolated pig-farm, and had found a herd of pigs, and dropped food for them. Then – 'And you'll never believe this,' each said – they had come to a place where a big jumble of uprooted trees and other rubbish, including what looked like a shed, had dammed the stream and formed a big pool.

On one side of this pool stood two great spotted pigs. And flying above the pool was a black-and-white duck. And in the middle of the pool was a man, a huge fat man from what they could see of him, struggling madly in the water; they could hear nothing because of the noise of the rotors, but they could see his mouth open in a shout for help before he went down again.

Then – 'It's true, I promise you,' each said – a little spotty piglet – 'odd-looking thing with a head too big for its body and funny feet' – dived off the dam into the pool, swam – 'yes, *swam*' – across it at tremendous speed, and seemed to say something to the two big pigs. They in turn put their heads down and tipped a stout piece of wood into the pool – 'a fencing stake it was'   and the piglet lined it up so the sharp end was pointing at the struggling man ('cross my heart'); then it swam round and pressed its snout to the blunt end ('Scout's honour'); the duck landed on top of the stake and flapped its wings like mad ('honest Injun'); and the piglet swam like billy-o, and the stake went

whizzing across the pool like a torpedo, and they got
to the man just as he was going down for the third
time, and he managed to grab the stake and hang on
to it, and so the duck and the amazing swimming
piglet saved his life ('see this wet, see this dry').

'But is all that really true, Dad?' said each of the
families.

'Of course it is,' said each father.

And of course it was.

As soon as the pigman had hit the water, Daggie
and Felicity knew that they must try to save him.
They could not simply let the servant drown.

'Shout to Father and Mammie to help!' yelled

Daggie, doing a racing dive into the pool.

'Quick!' cried Felicity, flying out towards the two big pigs. 'Find a heavyish bit of wood and get it into the water.'

'Here's a big old stake,' panted Mrs Barleylove, and, 'How about this, what?' grunted the Squire as they levered it out of the bankside rubbish.

'Let her go!' squeaked Daggie, and when he had lined up the stake, and Felicity had perched on its sharp end, he squealed, 'Full speed ahead!' and away they went.

The pool was smaller, the current less strong, and the waterfalls less menacing than they had been; but nonetheless the pigman, though now safe from drowning, was not safe from being swept down and away.

Then the miracle happened, to the amazement of the four animals who had been so intent that they had not noticed the hovering helicopter. Suddenly and dramatically its shadow fell across them, and its clatter burst upon their ears, and the water of the pool blossomed into a thousand catspaws under the downdraught of the rotors as the pilot dropped the craft to treetop height.

Leaning from the hatch, the observer directed him, while at the end of the rescue cable the winchman hung suspended over the pigman's head.

'Up a bit, on a bit, back a bit, down a bit!' and

then 'Hold it!' as the winchman slipped a rope beneath the pigman's arms and held up his hand to the watchers above.

Then the great strange bird lifted the big fat servant as easily as you would lift a spider on its thread, and drew him up into itself. Thoughtfully, it laid one more brown egg on the bank near the Squire and his wife, and then it turned and flew away.

The pool was quiet and its surface smooth again. The lifesaving fencing stake had gone down the waterfall, the bristles on the big pigs' backs lay flat again, and Daggie was beginning to control the shivering fit brought on by the excitement and terror of it all. Everybody reacted in a different way.

'It gobbled him up!' said Daggie with horror.

'Don't matter so long as you're all right,' said Mrs Barleylove with relief.

'In the name of St Anthony, what the devil was that thing?' said the Squire angrily.

'It was a helicopter,' said Felicity with amusement.

There was a pause while they all tucked into the pig-nuts.

'Extraordinary,' said the Squire with his mouth full. 'Damn feller's got no right to go flyin' off like that you know. Think we'll go home, when we've finished eatin'. Like to give the feller a piece of my mind. After all said and done, you saved his life, my son, you and your friend here, what?'

'Saved my life, saved my life,' babbled the pigman as he lay on the floor of the clattering machine. 'And to think I called 'em stupid, and iggerant, and 'orrible. And now see what they done for me. I'll make it up to 'em, I'll make it up to 'em. You see if I don't.'

'Yes, yes, old chap,' said the helicopter crew soothingly. 'Just you relax and don't worry. We'll soon have you in hospital.'

'Hospital?' said the pigman loudly, struggling to his wet feet. 'I don't want to go to no hospital. You get me back to the farm. I got a job to do. I got to get everything ready for 'em. When they come home.'

CHAPTER 18

MISSING

By evening the herd was comfortably full of food and the pigman once again ragingly hungry. He stood beside the helicopter which had landed in the yard, and stared at the concrete foundations where the meal-shed had stood. He was shocked and soaked, and his sluggish brain was hardly working at all. What thoughts he had were all of eating. But not pigmeat, not ever again, he said slowly to himself. Not ever again. Nor duck. Not after what they done for me. Not nohow.

And almost as though he were a mind-reader, the helicopter pilot said, 'I say, you must be pretty hungry, old chap. I mean, we had a jolly good breakfast of bacon and eggs' – the pigman shuddered – 'but you probably haven't eaten for days. Have my sandwiches. They're Spam.'

'I couldn't,' said the pigman in a low voice, and, thinking that he was nervous of accepting their hospitality, the observer said in a very friendly tone, 'Well I can offer you something better than Spam, old fellow. Have mine. They're duck paste.'

'Oh, I couldn't,' said the pigman, more miserably still.

'You're welcome to mine,' said the winchman, holding out a large packet of thick sandwiches, 'but they're nothing very special.'

'What are they?' asked the pigman in a tremulous voice.

'Marmite,' said the winchman, and then leapt back in surprise as, with a great grunt of delight, the pigman snatched the packet from his hands, tore off the wrapping, and stuffed the whole wad in his mouth.

The crew of the helicopter watched silently as the pigman chomped and chawed with his strong yellow tusks, his big nostrils flaring, his little eyes tight shut in ecstasy.

'No wonder he's fat as a pig,' thought the pilot.

'Talk about greedy as a pig,' thought the observer.

'Blowed if he doesn't look like a pig,' thought the winchman, as with a last snort of pleasure the pigman finished the Marmite sandwiches and ran his tongue over his three chins in search of crumbs.

And almost as though he were reading the crew's thoughts, the pigman suddenly shouted, 'Pigs!'

'What d'you mean?' cried the crew, jumping back nervously.

'Pigs. My pigs. Out there.' The pigman gestured towards Resthaven.

'They must be fair starved. Got to get grub to 'em. Got to get my meal-shed back somehow.'

They explained to him that they had dropped food, enough to be going on with, they thought, and then the pilot said, 'That hut thing we sighted – where we pulled you out of the water – is that your meal-shed?'

'That's her,' said the pigman.

'How did it get there?'

'She floated.'

'Well,' said the pilot. 'How about us towing the thing back for you? If it floated down, it might float back. No use to you down there.'

So they left the pigman with dry clothing, and lifted away downstream. On their way to the dam, they passed the black-and-white duck flying towards the farm.

Felicity landed on her perch in the alder tree and looked about her. In the distance she could see the herd in Resthaven. They were lying about in the sunshine, apparently contented. Way beyond them she could just make out the figures of the Squire and Mrs Barleylove sploshing homewards. Near to her, the pigman was hard at work sweeping the last of the water from the sties, and bringing dry bedding straw from the top of the barn where the flood had not reached it. He was a picture in navy blue overalls and flying boots. Everything's returning to normal, she thought to herself. Except for the meal-shed, but that's asking a bit much.

But it wasn't, for before long she heard the rattly voice of the great strange bird, and there beneath and behind it was the meal-shed, stately as a galleon,

coming slowly upstream on the end of a long tow-rope.

At the dam, both winchman and observer had gone down the cable while the pilot hovered, and had fastened ropes both around and under the shed as though tying up a giant parcel. Now, close by Felicity's alder tree, the winchman released the tow-rope, re-fastened the cable to the top of the parcel, and raised his hand.

Gradually the meal-shed rose out of the stream, timbers creaking, open door swinging, sailed over the buildings, and was lowered, gently, exactly, on to its foundations. The ropes were released and drawn up, and once again the flying machine dropped down into the yard.

'OK?' shouted the pilot to the pigman. 'All right now? All your pigs back?'

'I'll just check,' yelled the pigman, and he walked out into Resthaven.

Five minutes later he was back at a run, his big face white and his fat cheeks wobbling.

'My dag! My little dag!' he shouted. 'He's not come home!'

'Dag?' cried the pilot.

'Yes! The one who saved my life!' roared the pigman, and a couple of tears came out of his piggy eyes and ran down his cheeks and over the hills and valleys of his three chins.

'Oh, is that what he's called?' yelled the pilot. 'Well, don't you worry, old chap. We'll nip back and see where he's got to. He's probably swimming home,' and away they went downstream again.

CHAPTER 19

A SUDDEN
AWFUL FRIGHT

When the Squire and Mrs Barleylove had started home from the dam, they had given Daggie permission to go on ahead of them. They did not believe he could come to any harm on the fast-drying bank. He's a big boy now, and sensible, they said to each other.

But like any adventurous youngster, Daggie decided not to do what he had been told, but something much more exciting instead.

'Let them go home by land,' he said loudly as soon as he was out of earshot, 'I'm a swimming pig, and

I'm going to swim home.'

He hid himself until he saw the meal-shed sailing by, and until his mother and father had passed him and disappeared. Then he slipped into the water.

The current was still fairly strong but he was confident he could swim against it; still, he thought he would start in a quietish place, a deep inlet that was out of the main run of water. He glided out from the bank, but instead of going straight into his usual racing crawl, he decided to have a splash and a play. He put his head under, and found himself staring into a pair of cold hard eyes, set behind narrow wolf-jaws and backed by a long barred body.

Before he could move, there was an explosion in the depths beneath him, he felt a violent blow which almost lifted him out of the water, and the pike had clamped its jaws on the end of his snout.

In an agony of fear, Daggie pulled back with all his strength, thrashing and flailing in the water as he strove to get free. But the pike was bigger than he, and stronger than he, and its cruel teeth were tight in his tender nose, and he could not breathe. Gradually he grew weaker, and gradually the fierce fish pulled him deeper, and his mind began to spin, and a whole series of faces flashed across it, all in a split second. His Mammie's face, and the faces of his father the Squire, and his kind aunts, and the servant, and Felicity. And before his whirling senses became a blank black emptiness, there sounded in his ear a thin hard cry.

'I-zaak!' it seemed to say. 'I-zaak!'

When Daggie Dogfoot came to himself, there was still a face in front of him. But this time it was a real face, a live face, a round whiskery face wearing a look of deep anxiety. And out of it came a worried voice.

'Old pig! Old pig!' the voice said. 'You're all right, aren't you? You're all right? Now don't say you ain't 'cos you are.'

Daggie looked about him and found that he was lying in the grass by the brookside. He sicked up a lot of water and lay panting, his whole body shaking with shock.

'Ike!' he croaked. 'Oh, Ike! What happened? What was it? Oh, my nose! And the back of my neck!'

'What happened, old pig,' said Ike, 'was that you came pretty close to being drowned and eaten, and don't say you didn't 'cos you did. Your nose is sore because you've had a couple of dozen razor-sharp teeth stuck in it, and your neck's sore because I had to haul you out by the scruff.'

'But what was it, Ike? What was that dreadful fish?'

'Pike,' said Ike. 'That was a pike, old pig.'

'But it was so huge,' said Daggie. 'I never knew they were as big as that. Felicity never warned me.'

'She never knew either, old pig,' said Ike. 'That's the biggest ever. Lived in the mill-pond and got washed out when the sluice-gates burst. Dying to meet him, I've been, and now I've met him, *he's* dying!' and the otter threw back his head and shook with silent laughter.

Daggie staggered to his feet and looked down into the water. Floating there on its side was the long barred shape of the monster pike of the mill-pond, the wolf-jaws split wide in the gape of agony caused by the otter's death-bite. Between the dorsal fin and the tail was a terrible scooped-out gash.

'I broke his back, old pig,' said Ike, standing beside

the gazing piglet. 'And don't say I didn't 'cos I did.
Now I'll fetch him out and we'll eat the best of him.
I'll be laughing all the way to the bank!'

CHAPTER 20

'TIDDEN "MIGHT", 'TIS "CAN"!'

Daggie was very very full. He was also, suddenly, very tired, from the strain of all his adventures, and particularly the shock of the last of them. He flopped down on the bank and rolled over into a slight hollow, so that he lay upon his back, all four legs stuck up in the air. Immediately, he fell into the deepest of deep sleeps.

Minutes passed, and in the bright evening sunshine bees buzzed and a big fat bluebottle landed neatly on the staring eye of the dead pike.

Suddenly there came a wailing mewing noise from

the blue sky above, and Ike, looking up from the bushes where he was dozing, saw a solitary buzzard circling on wide wings over the sleeping piglet. It had come down from the high moors, feeding on the carcasses of drowned sheep.

The otter knew that buzzards were carrion-eating cowards, and he had no fears for Daggie's safety. If his friend did not wake, he thought, he would give it a sudden awful fright. He grinned happily.

The big hawk dropped lower. It could see below what appeared to be a very dead animal, whose belly was blown up like a drum and whose legs stuck out stiffly. Moreover, its nose was caked with dried blood.

The scavenger prepared to land, but at that moment it heard a loud noise in the distance, and a great strange bird with twinkling glassy eyes and wings that whirled above its body came clattering downstream. The buzzard flew away with a cry of alarm, and even the bold Ike slid out of the bushes and into the water, where he lay with only his mask showing and watched. The helicopter checked and the crew peered down.

'There he is!' shouted the observer. 'But dead as a button by the look of him. Something's got the poor little chap. Look at the blood on his snout.'

'We'd better pick him up,' the pilot said.

'Death of a Hero,' said the winchman.

All of a sudden the same thought occurred to the

three men of the Fleet Air Arm, as they hovered above the still-broad river in their blue machine with the proud letters 'R.N.' upon its side. They remembered the story of Nelson's last voyage, his coffin carried upon a barge up the Thames to the Admiralty.

'Tell you what,' said the pilot. 'We can't float him home in state, but we can fly him. After all he was quite unique, the one and only swimming pig. Let's give him the grandest possible return to his last resting-place.'

'On the end of the rescue cable, eh?' said the observer. 'So that the mourning multitudes can pay their respects?'

'That's it,' said the pilot. 'Remember the old saying – "pigs might fly!"' and the three young men grinned at each other.

'Well, let's make a proper job of it,' said the winchman. 'I'll go down and strap him on – I can adjust the harness – and then I'll wait here on the river bank and you can pick me up later when you've delivered him home.'

So down went the cable with the winchman, and he fitted the straps around the small spotty body, thinking as he did so that the piglet could not have been dead long, he was so warm. He raised his hand, and the helicopter lifted gently away with Daggie Dogfoot dangling thirty feet below it.

Until that moment – and only St Anthony knows how – Daggie had remained in his deepest of sleeps. Through the cries of the buzzard, and the rattling and downdraught of the flying machine, and even the harnessing of his body, he had slept on relentlessly. Indeed he had just begun to dream his old dream, of flying with his mother and father through a warm and milky sky, when the tightening of the straps and the rush of air at last wakened him to reality.

Twisting in the harness so that his little legs hung down, he saw below him, fast growing smaller, a man on the ground and an otter in the water, staring up at him. His ears flapped and his tail whirled, and in terrified surprise he kicked like mad with all four legs, his mouth wide open as he squealed with horror. The watchers, two above him, two below, could of course hear nothing of it, but they could see that the gallant hero was in fact very much alive. Three of them grinned their relief and pleasure, and the fourth one laughed so much and rocked about so wildly that eventually he sank below the water and swallowed some mouthfuls.

But once he had come to his senses and understood that he was safely anchored to the great bird above, Daggie stopped feeling so panic-stricken and began to look around. Below him, as they gained height for the homeward run, the river became a stream and the stream a trickle. Great trees shrank to the size of thistles, and far below him the swallows flew in ignorance of the miracle above. He opened wide his mouth again, but this time the unheard squeal was of excitement, of happiness, of triumph!

'Pigs might fly!' shouted Daggie, his accent growing broader as the thrill grew more keen. 'Thass wot thee said, A'ntie Gobblespud, thees-know! Tidden "might", 'tis "can"! Theseyer pig be flyin'! So look out, A'ntie, look out the rest of ee, look out Father, look out Mammie! WEEEEEEEEEEEEEE! Yur Oi come!'

CHAPTER 21

HOME AND DRY

Meanwhile back at the farm they were indeed looking out, every one of them. The Squire had brought the herd down into the yard and called the roll, and now everyone knew that Daggie was missing, Daggie who had somehow saved them all by going for help, summoning the great clattering bird, bringing back the servant and his meal-shed. They did not doubt that it was he who had now caused the waters to go down. Probably he could not just swim in them, but walk upon them too. But would he? Would they ever see him again?

At the distant sound of the approaching helicopter every head was raised. At first they could only make out the machine itself, coming up the line of the brook, a black dot in the eye of the westering sun. But as it drew nearer they could see below it a small figure and knew themselves to be looking at yet another miracle.

And now what rejoicing broke out among the Ploughbarrow herd! How the weaners waltzed and the store pigs sported and the fatteners frolicked!

'Love him!' shouted the eight aunts, shaking their floppy ears, 'if he ain't the cleverest ever!'

'Oh Squire!' cried Mrs Barleylove. 'Whatever's happening? Surely Daggie can't really be flying?'

The great boar looked at her and then up at this amazing son of theirs kicking and flapping and twirling away above them.

'By St Anthony!' bawled the Squire. 'He's doing better than that, m'dear. Must be something wrong with that damned thing doncherknow, and the boy's towing it in, butchered if he ain't!'

Once above the buildings, the pilot made his machine describe a couple of tight circles so that Daggie was whirled around in much larger circles, just as a boy whirls a conker on the end of its string. Felicity flew up to greet him, but he was travelling so fast that she could only catch his squeals of excitement each time he flashed by her on this most marvellous of roundabouts.

Now the helicopter was hovering steady, directly

above the yard, directly above the figure of the pigman in his new navy overalls waiting anxiously below. Gradually Daggie's circles grew smaller and slower, until at last he hung still like a plumb-bob. Gently, very gently, the pilot lowered the piglet. Gently, very gently, the piglet touched down. Gently, very gently, the pigman came forward to release the straps of the harness. To do so he needed to kneel down, and the herd of course was duly impressed that at long last the servant was showing a proper degree of respect.

'Hey you, Pigman. Scratch my back,' said Daggie Dogfoot. And the servant of course obeyed.

Above them all the pilot and the observer waved

their final farewells before clattering away into the sunset to pick up the winchman and set course for their base. And as they went down the stream a string of bubbles came up it, and as their racket died away a shrill clear whistle pierced the evening air, and a long low creature with a grinning whiskery face and a battery of sharp white teeth hauled out of the water by Felicity's alder and came to join the pigs.

Now everybody looked at the returned adventurer. And everybody saw his bloody nose, which only one of them knew the reason for. And everybody saw his curious puppy-like forefeet, which some of them knew about. But what everybody saw and everybody knew was that here in front of them was a Brave Hero, the only dag ever to be taken away and yet come back, who had risked his life on the swollen waters to swim for help. And that help had come, precious food from out of the skies, manna from heaven. Thanks to Daggie Dogfoot, they were all home and dry.

Then the herd turned and moved contentedly away to the familiar comfort of their sties and pens and the pleasant anticipation of a good supper to come. The otter slipped back into the brook and the duck followed him. Only Mrs Barleylove and the servant still stood by the hero. The pigman brushed a great hand across his face and sniffed a bit.

'Drat me!' he said softly, and 'Dang me!' and

'Blast me!' And he too turned away and went to prepare the meal.

'Happy, my baby?' said Mrs Barleylove gently.

'Oh yes,' said Daggie, 'but Mammie, there's just one thing I'd like to do before bedtime. Can I have a swim?'

'Of course,' said his mother, and together they walked down through Resthaven to the old pool below the high bank, where the water was almost back to its usual level. The kingfisher sat once again upon his perching root, brilliant in the last light of the setting sun, and the moorhens murmured happily in the reeds. Two bathers were already in the pool.

'Coming in, Daggie?' called Felicity as she twirled and splashed in a shower of golden drops, but he was already gone, running to the top of the slope to prepare for the downhill take-off. 'What about you, missus?' said the duck mischievously. 'Going to have a go?'

'Blimey, old duck,' said Ike softly, 'that'd be a sight to see, and don't say it wouldn't 'cos it would!' and he opened his mouth very wide and rocked to and fro.

But Mrs Barleylove wasn't listening. She gave an absent-minded grunt and moved away up the field to the spot where the old oak had stood, her eyes upon her son.

And now Daggie Dogfoot turned and began to

run downhill at great speed, faster, faster, faster, till at last he leaped out over the high bank of the stream, and disappeared from her sight. What clever things her brilliant baby was doing in his favourite element she could not see, but she could hear the joyful squeals and the flutey whistles and the soft quot-quot-quotting noises, as he dived and splashed and raced with his friends.

And high above she could hear the cries of the homecoming rooks, as they circled in the warm air and marvelled at the miraculous skills of the amazing swimming pig.

'Cor!' they shouted to one another in awestruck admiration. 'Cor! Cor! Cor!'